UNWELCOME VISITOR

In the abandoned building, the Hardys found a room filled with cardboard cartons.

His adrenaline racing, Frank walked over to the closest box. "Tape reels," he said. "These could be the counterfeit components."

Joe was peering at a stack of open boxes at the far end of the room. "Those look like they might be video game cartridges."

"Excellent!" Frank said. "We've got the proof we need." He began to cross the room to check out the cartridges, but Joe's voice stopped him.

"Frank." Joe's voice had taken on an urgency. "We've got company."

Frank whirled around. Standing in the doorway was a muscular young man. Frank recognized him immediately—it was the guy who'd stolen Mariko's bag! In his hand was a long, wooden pole, and he was swinging it with the practiced grace of someone who knew how to kill.

Nancy Drew & Hardy Boys SuperMysteries

DOUBLE CROSSING
A CRIME FOR CHRISTMAS
SHOCK WAVES
DANGEROUS GAMES
THE LAST RESORT
THE PARIS CONNECTION
BURIED IN TIME
MYSTERY TRAIN
BEST OF ENEMIES
HIGH SURVIVAL
NEW YEAR'S EVIL
TOUR OF DANGER

Available from ARCHWAY Paperbacks

TOUR OF DANGER

Carolyn Keene

AN ARCHWAY PAPERBACK
Published by POCKET BOOKS
New York London Toronto Sydney Tokyo Singapore

This book is a work of fiction. Names, characters, places, and incidents are either the product of the author's imagination or are used fictitiously. Any resemblance to actual events or locales or persons, living or dead, is entirely coincidental.

AN ARCHWAY PAPERBACK *Original*

An Archway Paperback published by
POCKET BOOKS, a division of Simon & Schuster Inc.
1230 Avenue of the Americas, New York, NY 10020

Produced by Mega-Books of New York, Inc.

ISBN: 0-671-67468-4

First Archway Paperback printing April 1992

10 9 8 7 6 5 4 3 2 1

Cover illustration by Frank Morris

Printed in the U.S.A.

IL 6+

TOUR OF DANGER

Chapter One

"DO YOU SEE what I see?" Nancy Drew whispered to her boyfriend, Ned Nickerson. Bess Marvin, Nancy's good friend, was standing in front of the Journeys East tour office, and the sight of Bess's back fascinated Nancy.

"Bess," Nancy asked tentatively, "what is that sticking out of your head?"

Bess turned to face them, a smile on her face. "Chopsticks," she answered matter-of-factly. "Black lacquered chopsticks. Japanese women have been pinning their hair up this way for centuries."

"Oh," said Nancy, remembering pictures of Japanese women in kimonos, their long black hair swept up and held in place with what looked like chopsticks. Somehow the effect wasn't quite the same with Bess's blond bun.

"When in Rome—" Bess started to quote.

Ned leaned conspiratorially toward Nancy. "Should we tell her she's going to Tokyo, Japan?" he half whispered.

"I think she knows," Nancy answered with a laugh. She was glad Bess had agreed to join her on a two-week tour of Tokyo.

Ned unloaded three suitcases from the trunk of his car. As usual the two big ones belonged to Bess. Nancy had managed to fit all her things into one medium-size suitcase. Ned carried the two large bags into the crowded Journeys East office and headed for the check-in counter, where seven long lines stretched back toward the door.

"I hope we get checked in before the bus leaves for the airport," Bess said worriedly.

"We'll make it; our flight isn't for hours," Nancy said, brushing her reddish blond hair away from her eyes. "But I wonder if our tour is actually leaving today," Nancy said.

"What do you mean?" Bess asked. "Of course we're leaving today."

"Bess, you and Ned and I are the only people in this room under sixty. This is obviously a senior citizens' tour."

"You know, you'd make a first-rate detective,

Ms. Drew," Ned said, his brown eyes sparkling with approval.

Nancy rolled her eyes and swatted him lightly on the arm. She was, in fact, a first-rate amateur detective.

"Well, we've got the date and time right. There must be some mistake," Bess said, worried.

When Nancy and Bess reached the front of the line and showed a weary clerk their tickets, his eyes widened. "There's definitely a mistake here," he said apologetically. "Your tour left for Tokyo yesterday."

He quickly added, "But don't worry. We can put you on today's flight with the seniors, and you can join your group tomorrow. All our groups stay in the same hotel."

With that, Bess and Nancy went to board the bus for the airport. First, though, Nancy found herself in her tall, handsome boyfriend's arms, gazing into his dark eyes and wondering why she was about to spend two weeks away from him.

"I'm going to miss you," he said softly.

"Me, too. I mean, I'll miss you."

Ned shook his head. "I know it's useless to say this, but try not to get mixed up in anything dangerous. Okay?"

"Ned, this is a vacation," Nancy told him

firmly. "I'm not going to Tokyo to solve a mystery."

"Yeah, right," he teased. "When have I heard that one before?" Ned reached out one hand and lightly ran his thumb along her cheekbone. Then he bent and gave her a lingering kiss. "I'll see you in two weeks."

Nancy nodded, breathless. At the moment two weeks seemed like an awfully long time.

"We will be landing in Narita Airport in approximately thirty minutes," the pilot announced.

Nancy yawned and stretched her long, slender frame. It was almost three o'clock in the afternoon on Thursday, Tokyo time. She'd lost track of how many hours they had been in the air, but it felt like forever.

Beside her, Bess opened one eye. "Are we there?" she asked sleepily.

"Another half hour," Nancy answered.

Bess sat up with a start and immediately began fumbling with her hair. "I must look awful," she said.

"No worse than the rest of us," said the gray-haired woman on Nancy's right. She and Nancy had talked while Bess was sleeping. Her name was Adele Olson, and she and her husband, John, were part of the seniors' tour. "Besides, I don't really think it will matter,"

Mrs. Olson went on. "We're going straight to the hotel to sleep off our jet lag."

"But think of who we might meet on the way," Bess said.

"Who?" Nancy wondered.

"Someone wonderful," Bess said in a dreamy voice.

Mrs. Olson laughed and patted her husband's hand. "I met my someone wonderful thirty-five years ago."

"Well, thank you," said Mr. Olson, who was seated next to his wife in the wide center section. He peered at Bess and said, "Nancy tells us you're quite a shopper."

Bess grinned. "Born to shop, that's me."

"Well, maybe you can give us some advice. We're looking for a gift for our daughter, who's graduating from medical school this fall," Mr. Olson said. "Adele thinks we should bring back a camera for her, but I was thinking that maybe a strand of pearls—"

Nancy listened contentedly as Bess and the Olsons discussed shopping until they landed safely.

As the girls emerged from customs, a handsome young man who was about twenty approached them. His hair was worn long in back, and he had on jeans, a button-down striped shirt, and an earring in one ear.

"Ms. Drew, Ms. Marvin?" he inquired in unaccented American English.

"That's us," said Bess, who was struggling with her suitcases. "I'm Bess Marvin and this is my friend Nancy Drew."

"May I?" the young man asked, holding out his hands for Bess's bags. "My name is Hiro Katayama. I'm the guide for your tour group. Since Journeys East goofed on your reservations, I've been sent to escort you to the hotel."

Bess smiled at him. "If you'll carry my bags, you can escort me anywhere."

Hiro smiled back at her, and Nancy marveled at Bess's ability to charm any good-looking guy she met.

"Were you born here?" Nancy asked Hiro as they boarded the bus for the hotel. "You speak English like an American."

"I grew up in Kyoto," he replied. "But our next-door neighbors were Americans who had twin sons my age. I spent so much time playing at their house that I soon spoke fluent English. Now I'm in college in Tokyo, studying English and history."

"You run tour groups in your free time?" Bess asked. "You must be pretty busy."

Hiro grimaced. "I ran out of money, so I took half a year off from school to work. It's been fun. I especially think *this* tour will be great because all the people are about my age."

Nancy found her attention drifting away from the conversation because she was captivated by the glimpses of Japan through the bus windows. When the bus pulled into the heart of Tokyo, she was in awe. The city was bigger, more crowded, and even more hectic than she'd imagined. Giant neon signs flashed from every building, and gleaming modern skyscrapers towered over tiny shops. The streets were mazes of traffic and people.

"This is crazier than New York," Bess murmured.

"Probably," Hiro said. "Tokyo is a city of contradictions—the very old and the very new exist side by side. It's totally modern, and yet a lot of what happens here is guided by traditions that go back to our medieval period."

The bus stopped at a traffic light, and Nancy idly watched a group of young men in business suits leave one of the modern office buildings.

"Bess," she said, her eyes wide with disbelief, "do you see who I see?"

"Frank and Joe Hardy!" Bess exclaimed. The Hardy brothers were two young detectives who were friends of Nancy and Bess. Nancy had teamed up with them to solve mysteries more than a few times.

"Friends of yours?" Hiro asked politely.

"Yes," Nancy answered. She didn't mention that the Hardys were probably working on a case. Nothing but a case could usually get Joe into a suit. I hope I can contact them, she thought.

Hiro escorted the girls into the lobby of their hotel. "All you have to do is check in," he told them. "Someone will see you to your room and we'll send up some dinner. That way you can go right to sleep. Our tour begins at eight tomorrow morning," he went on. "We all eat lunch together, but breakfast is on your own. The hotel coffee shop is fairly trustworthy."

"Sounds good," Nancy said, stifling a yawn. She was feeling more jet-lagged than she'd expected and couldn't wait to sleep.

"Where did the Olsons go?" Bess asked after Hiro left them.

Nancy took in the crowded hotel lobby. "Maybe they're over there," she said, nodding to the concierge's desk, where a group of seniors was gathered.

"No," Bess said. "The sign over there says To Narita Airport. That group must be going back to the States." She turned around. "There they are!" she cried, waving to them before going to the desk to check in.

Nancy's attention had remained on the concierge's desk, where a frail, elderly woman was handing a beautiful blue-and-white ceramic vase to the concierge. Her hand trembled and the vase slipped from her fingers.

Nancy's mouth fell open in amazement as the vase shattered against the floor and dozens of perfect, round white pearls skittered across the lobby.

Chapter Two

"MY VASE!" the elderly woman cried. "What in the world . . ." Her voice trailed off, and she continued to stare wordlessly at the cascade of pearls.

Nancy hurried to the woman's side and heard her murmur something about her arthritis as she bent over to pick up the pieces. "Here," Nancy said, "let me help you."

"I wouldn't touch anything if I were you," a middle-aged blond man in a brown business suit said. Flanking him were two other men.

The blond man flashed a badge at the woman. "Stuart Hartwell, Special Investigator, CIA." He nodded to the two men at his side. "I'm working in cooperation with the Tokyo Police. And you are—"

"Lettie Aldridge," the woman answered. She nervously patted her short gray hair into place.

"Do you want to tell us where you got those pearls, Ms. Aldridge?" Mr. Hartwell asked.

"I don't know," the elderly woman replied. "I suppose they must have been in the vase."

One of the Japanese officers began collecting the pearls and pieces of the vase, placing them in separate envelopes. The other officer kept the crowd back.

"Was that your vase?" Mr. Hartwell asked.

"I bought it as a gift for my sister."

"And you had no idea it contained a fortune in pearls?"

"Certainly not!" Ms. Aldridge replied indignantly.

Mr. Hartwell sighed. "I'm afraid you'll have to come with us, Ms. Aldridge."

The woman acted terrified. "I'm—I don't know what—" she stammered.

"Can't you tell her why?" Nancy intervened.

Mr. Hartwell glanced at the pearls. "We've been trying to crack a pearl-smuggling operation for the last six months," he answered. "And we just got our first big break."

"You mean this vase?" Nancy asked.

"Who are you?" Hartwell asked brusquely, fixing her with a stern gaze.

"My name is Nancy Drew, and—"

"Any relation to Ms. Aldridge here?"

"No, we just met, but—"

"Then I'm going to have to ask you to stay out of this," Mr. Hartwell said. "Come along, Ms. Aldridge."

Nancy tried one more time. "Wait a minute," she began. "I'm sure this can all be explained—"

"I'm sorry, but Ms. Aldridge will have to come with us. You'll excuse us, Ms. Drew?"

Nancy watched helplessly as the woman was led across the lobby. She glanced down then and saw a piece of the broken vase under the concierge's desk. Nancy scooped it up. She wasn't sure what good it would do, but maybe it would help her to prove Lettie Aldridge's innocence.

"We're all checked in, and our luggage is on the way up to our room," Bess announced, coming to stand beside Nancy. "What was going on over here?"

"An innocent old lady is being arrested for pearl smuggling," Nancy said grimly. She nodded to the far end of the lobby, where Lettie Aldridge stood surrounded by police. "I wish I could help her."

Bess nodded across the lobby. "Maybe Hiro can," she said.

The tour guide was already making his way toward Ms. Aldridge.

"Come on," Bess said, "let's see what happens."

Nancy and Bess stood a short distance away from the group and listened.

Hiro had begun speaking in rapid Japanese to the two police officers. Then he spoke in English to Detective Hartwell. "I'm sure there's been a mistake," he said calmly. "Ms. Aldridge has been part of my tour group for the past two weeks. She would never steal, and she also has a heart condition. Can't you question her here instead of taking her to the police station?"

The police conferred and agreed to Hiro's suggestion. Nancy listened, fascinated, as Mr. Hartwell explained to Hiro that six months ago there was a large pearl theft from one of the pearl farms on the Kii peninsula. Some of the pearls were recently traced to the United States. Since then the Tokyo police and the CIA had been working together to crack the smuggling operation. "We think it may be operating out of this hotel," Mr. Hartwell finished.

"And you—you think *I* had something to do with it?" Ms. Aldridge said, outraged.

"You were about to bring a vase with pearls into the United States," Hartwell pointed out dryly.

"But I didn't know—"

"Where did you buy the vase?" he asked.

"Kyoto, I think. Or was it Tokyo?" She looked to Hiro for confirmation.

He shrugged and said, "Our group has been

in both cities and purchased souvenirs in numerous shops."

"Think, Ms. Aldridge," Mr. Hartwell urged.

There was a long moment of silence before the elderly woman said brightly, "I think the shop was near a shrine!"

"Great," Hartwell muttered. "That really narrows it down. There are shrines on every other corner in Japan."

Ms. Aldridge's face fell, and Hiro said, "Please. You are offending her. She is trying to help."

"All right." Mr. Hartwell tried again. "What did this shop look like?"

Confusion crossed Ms. Aldridge's face. "I can't remember."

Once again the police officers spoke to Hiro.

"Ms. Aldridge, the police aren't going to arrest you," Hiro translated. "But they would like you to remain here for a few days in case they need to ask you questions."

"But I'm supposed to fly home today!" the woman protested, her voice shaking. "My sister will be waiting at the airport and—"

"We can call your sister," Hiro broke in gently. "I'll arrange another room for you at the hotel."

"I'm afraid you don't have a choice," Hartwell added.

Ms. Aldridge nodded, and Nancy could see

that she was fighting back tears. Nancy waited until the police had left before she and Bess joined Hiro and Ms. Aldridge.

"Are you okay?" Nancy asked the elderly woman.

Ms. Aldridge nodded. "It's just that I was counting on going home today."

"I know," Hiro said kindly.

A young man whom Hiro had been talking to earlier called out to him just then. Nancy saw that he, too, wore a Journeys East badge. Kenji Ueda was his name. Kenji and Hiro's talk lasted only a few seconds at the end of which Hiro seemed to be angry. He was composed when he turned back to the Americans.

"I'm sorry," he said, "there's a phone call I have to take." He took Ms. Aldridge's hand. "I'll arrange for a new room for you in a few minutes. Will you be all right?"

"We'll stay with her until then," Nancy volunteered as Hiro and Kenji walked off. "My name is Nancy Drew, and this is my friend Bess Marvin."

Ms. Aldridge nodded at them distractedly. "Pearls," she murmured. "That vase had pearls in it—"

"Where were they exactly?" Nancy asked.

"I have no idea. I thought it was an empty vase."

Nancy shook her head, thinking. "They must

have been hidden in a false bottom or something."

She thought of the broken piece of ceramic in her purse. "I wish I could take a look at the rest of that vase," she said, thinking out loud.

"Why?" Ms. Aldridge asked.

"Nancy's a detective," Bess explained.

"I'd like to help you," Nancy added.

"Oh." Mrs. Aldridge smiled and held out her hand. "In that case, please call me Lettie."

Nearly an hour later, after seeing Lettie settled in her new room, Nancy and Bess arrived in their room.

"Oh," Bess said with a disappointed sigh.

"What's wrong?" Nancy asked, taking in the simple, modern furnishings.

"It looks just like an American hotel room," Bess complained. She plopped down on a bed. "I thought our room would have those sliding paper screens and straw mats on the floor and we'd be sleeping on futons."

"I think my guidebook says that you only find that kind of room in the traditional inns," Nancy said as she kicked off her shoes. "They're called *ryokans.*"

Seeing Bess's disappointment, she added, "Maybe you and I can take a day off and go stay in a *ryokan.*"

"Definitely," said Bess, brightening. She went

to the desk, where two black lacquered boxes and two sets of chopsticks were sitting. "These must be the dinners Hiro sent up." She opened one lid and stared down at a colorful array of rectangular wedges.

"Sushi," Nancy pronounced, checking her dinner box.

"You mean, raw fish?" Bess sounded a little sick.

Nancy nodded. "It's a delicacy," she said. "Try it."

Bess was doubtful. Hesitantly, she picked up a piece of sushi and bit into it. A second later a smile lit her face. "You know something? I think I'm going to like Japan." She gave a soft giggle. "I already like one of its citizens."

"You mean Hiro?" Nancy asked, raising a brow.

"Wasn't he great with Ms. Aldridge?"

"He was," Nancy agreed. "But I disagree with him that the vase filled with pearls was a freak accident."

"Uh-oh," Bess said. "I know that gleam in your eye. You've only been in Japan a few hours and already you're on the case."

Laughing, Nancy said, "You know me too well. So let's say the police are right, and there is a smuggling ring operating out of the hotel. Well, smugglers use mules—people to carry their illegal goods out of the country. Often mules are paid couriers, but sometimes they don't even know they're carrying the contraband."

"And you think Lettie was one of the mules who don't know they're carrying the stuff?"

Nancy nodded, her face grim. "And that means there are probably others. I'm going to need some information on the seniors' tours, and I also want to stop in a library to see what I can find out about that robbery on the Kii peninsula."

"Then what?" Bess asked.

"Then we stop this thing before some other innocents—like the Olsons—become the pearl smugglers' next unwilling couriers!"

Chapter Three

EARLY FRIDAY MORNING Frank Hardy stood in the warehouse of Amsa Elite, the high-tech branch of Amsa Electronics Company.

According to the information on his clipboard, there were three thousand Amsa Elite CD players waiting to be packed into cartons and shipped to various U.S. distributors.

"Everything okay, Frank-san?" asked a thin young man holding another clipboard.

"Just dandy," Frank replied.

The young man's expression was perplexed. "Dandy?"

"Uh—that means great," Frank explained.

Isao Matsuda was the only other trainee in Amsa's shipping department who was fluent in English. Their supervisor, Mr. Hamaguchi, had immediately teamed up the two boys. Frank wasn't sure whether Isao was meant to be his guardian angel or his watchdog, but he was glad to work with someone who spoke English.

"So." Isao pointed to the list on Frank's clipboard. "You understand we must ship all these CD players today? They cannot be late."

"I'll get right on it." Frank watched Isao as he moved on. Why, he wondered, did Isao always seem so nervous?

Frank consulted his list and began to put together an order for seventy-five CD players to be sent to a St. Louis distributor. Frank had always daydreamed about owning an Amsa Elite stereo system. For anyone into high-tech equipment, the name Amsa Elite meant the best electronic components in the world. Now here he was, packing them by the thousands, and no closer to owning one than before.

Then again, he wasn't working as an Amsa trainee in order to get stereo equipment. Jim Yamada, the head of Amsa's American operations and a friend of Frank's father, had called Frank and Joe in to help him find out who was replacing Amsa Elite components with second-rate substitutes. Amsa's reputation in America had suffered recently because of the substitutions. Frank and Joe were working undercover in the company's trainee program.

What he really needed to do, thought Frank,

was open up one of the CD players and take a look at the parts. He glanced around the huge warehouse. There was no real place to hide, but the other shipping department trainees were all absorbed in packing their own orders.

Edging himself between two huge stacks of boxes, Frank helped himself to one of the CD players. He used his pocketknife to pry off the side of the sleek, black Amsa casing. Being careful not to disturb anything, he examined the neatly assembled components.

He gave a low whistle. None of them bore the tiny crescent within a circle, Amsa's trademarked symbol. He'd found a counterfeit!

"Frank-san?" Isao was calling. "How many cartons do you have ready?"

"Give me a minute and I'll count," he called back, quickly reassembling the CD player and slipping it into its box. He gave Isao the required count and went back to work.

"It's a good thing the tour covers lunch and dinner," Bess said as she and Nancy left the hotel coffee shop after breakfast.

"No kidding," Nancy agreed. "I can't believe a cup of coffee here costs more than an entire lunch back in the States."

"The guidebooks said Tokyo was expensive, but this is ridiculous," said Bess. "I hope I can afford a silk kimono."

Nancy glanced at her watch. "I want to make a quick stop in the gift shop before we meet our group."

"I'm looking for a blue-and-white vase," Nancy told the woman in the hotel shop. She took out the ceramic shard she'd picked up in the lobby the night before and held it out. "Do you have one with a pattern like this?"

The woman shook her head. "I'm sorry," she told Nancy. "Perhaps you will find it in another store."

"Nan, we've got to meet the others now," Bess reminded her. They found their tour group assembled near the entrance. Hiro introduced them to the others.

"This," he said, nodding to a tall, good-looking, dark-haired boy, "is Gary Leontes."

Gary darted a smile at Nancy and Bess, but the petite blond girl at his side didn't look nearly so friendly. Hiro introduced her as Wendy Wohl.

"This is Margot Harrison," he continued, indicating a graceful young woman whose jet black hair was in cornrow braids. "Margot is a dancer. And this is Michael Ryder."

The thin, gawky young man with glasses didn't even acknowledge them. He was peering intently through a video camera, which was pointed at a plant in the lobby.

Hiro glanced at his watch. "I'm sorry, but we have a bus to catch now. The Imperial Palace is our first stop."

Bess moved ahead to walk beside Hiro. As Bess laughed at something Hiro said, Margot turned to Nancy and asked, "Does she have a crush on our guide? Already?"

"It's possible," Nancy said diplomatically.

Margot laughed. "Then she's got good taste. Hiro's a real sweetie. Kenji's nice, too, but Hiro could charm the stars out of the sky."

He's certainly charmed Bess and Margot, Nancy thought as she boarded the bus. She was surprised when Gary Leontes took the empty seat next to her.

"Welcome," he said. "I heard about your mix-up on the flights. That must have been rough."

"It wasn't that bad," Nancy told him. "What did we miss yesterday?"

Gary rolled his eyes. "We went to a tea ceremony that was less thrilling than a checker game."

Nancy bit back a smile and noticed that Gary's eyes were a very light hazel, almost yellow gold against his tanned skin.

"So what made you decide to come to Japan?" Gary asked her.

"Sumo wrestling," Nancy deadpanned.

"In that case," he said, smiling at her, "I think you'll find Japan very interesting."

Twenty minutes later Nancy followed her group across a stone bridge and through the acres of parkland that surrounded the Imperial Palace, the official residence of Japan's imperial family.

In spite of the beautiful views, Nancy's mind was on Lettie Aldridge. She had to do something to help her. Where did this case really start? Nancy wondered. With the theft of the pearls six months ago, she decided. Which meant that she needed to find out about that theft. During the free time Journeys had scheduled for later that day, she'd find a library and do some research.

Hiro's voice snapped Nancy back to the present. The group was now facing one of the enormous palace walls. "This was originally the site of a fortress built by Lord Ota Dokan in 1457," he was explaining. "At that time Tokyo was called Edo, and this was the center of the city. The fortress was abandoned when Lord Ota was assassinated."

Hiro paused, grinning. "Unfortunately there's a lot of that sort of thing in Japan's history. In 1590, when Ieyasu Tokugawa was about to become shogun—the military head of state—he decided this would be a perfect site for his new castle. But he had no wish to end up like Lord Ota, so he enclosed the castle in a triple system of moats and canals. He also added ninety-nine gates, twenty-one watch towers, and twenty-eight armories."

Gary whistled. "That dude was serious about security!"

Hiro gave him a level gaze. "The 'way of the warrior' has always been taken very seriously in Japan, even in contemporary times. Within the palace walls, in addition to tennis courts, stables, a silkworm factory, and a hospital, there's also an air-raid shelter."

"That sounds like an awful lot of stuff for one family," Bess observed.

"Ah," Hiro said, smiling at her. "That's because when we say imperial family, we mean the two hundred and forty-five families who make up the official imperial family. The palace grounds are like a self-contained village."

"When do we go inside?" Wendy wanted to know.

"We don't," Hiro answered. "The palace isn't open to the public, and the palace gardens are open only two days a year. But these grounds are worth seeing. This way, please."

"What do you think?" Gary asked, moving up beside Nancy.

Nancy shrugged. "It seems like the shoguns

spent their entire lives plotting against one another."

"Well, I think the whole place is a rip-off," Wendy said, coming up between them. "What kind of tourist attraction doesn't let you inside?"

"The palace wasn't designed to be a tourist attraction," Gary said patiently. "It's where people live."

"Well, people live in the White House and we get to tour that," Wendy retorted, swiping a wayward strand of blond hair from her face.

Gary seemed embarrassed, and Nancy wondered just what their relationship was.

She was already sorting through the different personalities of the group. Margot got along with everyone. Michael was oblivious to anything that didn't pass through the lens of his video camera. Wendy didn't seem to like anyone except Gary. And as far as Nancy could tell, Bess was memorizing Hiro's every word. As for Gary—Nancy hadn't figured him out yet.

"Oh look," Bess cried as they left the palace grounds. She nodded toward a bearded man in a black kimono who sat at a folding table on the sidewalk. "I saw a picture just like that in one of the guidebooks. Is that man a palm reader?"

Hiro frowned. "That's what he'd like you to believe."

"Well, I thought the Imperial Palace was

boring," Wendy announced. "So we ought to do something fun—like have our fortunes told."

Hiro responded quickly. "You may be wasting your money—"

"It's *my* money," Wendy said. She marched up to the old man and demanded, "Do you speak English?"

"Enough," he replied, then quoted her a price.

Wendy gave him the money and held out her palm. The fortune-teller took it in his, studied it a moment, then nodded his head. "You are very difficult to please," he began. "You will have a great deal of money, and you will have everything you need to be content."

Pleased with her fortune, Wendy withdrew her hand.

"I'm next," Bess said, paying the man and offering her palm.

The fortune-teller spoke as soon as her hand was in his. "Love rules you," he said. "There will always be romance in your life. Sometimes two loves will conflict, but you will choose the right one."

Bess's face was bright red, but her blue eyes were sparkling with pleasure.

Margot was next, and the old man predicted a future filled with travel for her. "Oh, I hope that means I join a dance company that tours," Margot said.

Gary was told that people would always underestimate him, but he would prove his worth. Michael videotaped the fortunes but did not offer his hand.

"Come on, Nan," Bess urged, "it's your turn now."

Nancy was as skeptical of fortune-telling as Hiro was, but she was also curious. After all, the old man had pegged Bess pretty accurately. "All right," she agreed, paying the man and holding out her right hand.

The old man took her hand in his. His skin felt cool and crinkly, almost like paper. His eyes met hers for the briefest flicker of time. He held her hand for what seemed a long time, then at last he shrugged, dropped her palm, and said, "I'm sorry, what is in your palm is not clear."

"I don't believe that," Nancy said quietly. She held her hand out to him again. "Please," she said, "tell me what you see."

Reluctantly the old man took her hand. This time Nancy felt an irrational tingle of apprehension.

"You are in very great danger here," he said simply. "You must leave Japan at once."

Chapter Four

FRANK EMERGED FROM the warehouse at lunchtime, blinking against the bright spring sun. He squinted and recognized his brother's muscular frame by the warehouse door.

"So, how goes it in shipping?" Joe asked, shrugging uncomfortably in his suit jacket.

"I found one of the counterfeit CD players," Frank reported as they left the Amsa compound. "Which means the switch is happening here, not in any of the foreign ports, and it's got to be an inside job."

Joe ran a hand through his thick blond hair. "You only found one of the counterfeits?"

"I didn't exactly have a chance to open all the CD players," Frank told him. "Isao has us on this panic deadline. Either we ship every piece in there by the end of the day or the world comes to an end."

"Mmm," said Joe. He turned down the street and began walking toward the skyscraper that served as Amsa International's headquarters. "By the way, lunch is postponed," he informed Frank. "Mr. Yamada has invited us for a chat."

Inside the skyscraper the boys were ushered into the office of Jim Yamada, one of Amsa's senior vice presidents and head of American operations. Mr. Yamada divided his time between Amsa's Tokyo and San Francisco offices.

Frank was immediately impressed by Yamada's sparse, elegant office. The man was small with graying hair and stood gazing out the wall of windows at downtown Tokyo.

"Come in," he said, without turning to face the Hardys. "I was called here from my San Francisco office, so I thought I'd check in with you." When he turned to face them, Frank was reminded that for a small man, Yamada radiated tremendous authority.

Mr. Yamada cleared his throat. "About your investigation—I realize you've been here only a week, but have you made any progress?"

"I only had a chance to check out one of the CD players so far, but it was definitely one of the counterfeits. None of the components had the Amsa trademark."

"Just as I thought," said Mr. Yamada, nodding soberly. "This is an inside job, and you two are the only ones I can trust."

"What about the Tokyo police?" Joe asked.

"They sent undercover cops for a week. After that they were reassigned to 'more pressing matters.' I can't trust local private eyes—it would be too easy to hire someone who could be bought off."

He made a small bow, which the boys returned, and gestured for them to sit down. "Please accept my apologies. I have not properly welcomed you to Japan. How is it for you here? I regret that, aside from my niece, you are the only American trainees at present. I know it is hard to come into a foreign country with a difficult language, fit in as employees, *and* solve a case. Are your coworkers treating you well?"

"Well enough," Frank said.

"When they speak English," Joe added more bluntly. "To be honest, we feel like outsiders."

"You are," Yamada said. "That's precisely why you're my only hope of getting to the bottom of this. Until it's solved I can't trust any of my own employees. It is essential that no one suspect you are working for me." Mr. Yamada sat down at his desk. "Now that we know the counterfeits are being shipped from our own warehouse, we must discover how they get there."

Frank leaned forward in his chair. "I pulled

up the past year's computer shipping files on Amsa Elite CD players, but I couldn't find anything suspicious in the records."

"Which means that someone involved tampered with the computer records," Joe said.

"You have a suspect?" Mr. Yamada asked.

Joe nodded. "Tadashi Kamura in my department, research and development, can do anything with a computer."

Mr. Yamada frowned and made a steeple with his fingers. "Your supervisor, Mr. Okata, thinks very highly of Kamura. He says he's never seen so much talent or loyalty in a trainee."

Frank thought about mentioning Isao as a suspect, then rejected the idea. So far Isao hadn't done anything more suspicious than act nervous. Instead Frank said, "We need to find out where the fakes are being assembled. There's got to be someplace where they're switching parts."

"It's not in any of the Amsa buildings," Mr. Yamada assured them. "I have too many security guards."

"If someone is switching inferior goods for the real ones, then what's happening to the real ones?" Joe wanted to know.

"I suspect the real products are being sold on the black market. What I want to know is who is capable of counterfeiting our goods and then substituting the false ones," Yamada wondered.

He removed a file from a desk drawer and opened it to reveal a stack of newspaper clippings. "Forty of our machines with counterfeit parts were just discovered by a major electronics chain in Chicago. And a hundred more were found in Barcelona. If this goes on, Amsa Elite's reputation will be ruined."

Mr. Yamada gave a weary sigh. "You must do the most you can in the next two weeks. You will be rotated to other departments then, just like all the other trainees." His gaze settled on Joe, and for the first time there was a trace of humor in his expression. "Tell me," he said softly, "how is my niece Mariko doing? She is also in your trainee program, right?"

Frank wasn't sure why, but Joe hesitated a moment before answering. "She's fine. Mariko's doing just fine."

Joe returned to the brightly lit wing that served as Amsa's research and development department. At the end of the wing were the cubicles where the engineers who designed new products worked. The trainees all sat in one large open area close by.

A thin, balding man stuck his head out of the small office at the back of the trainees' area. Joe bowed to him.

"You are late from lunch," said his supervisor, Mr. Okata, in heavily accented English.

"Sumimasen," Joe replied, hoping he'd used the right form of apology. The Japanese had dozens of ways of saying "I'm sorry."

Okata did not look forgiving. "What is your reason for being late?"

Joe thought fast. "My brother and I were called in to see Mr. Yamada," he explained. "Since we're Americans, he wanted to welcome us here."

Mr. Okata raised his eyebrows but said nothing. Giving a short bow, he retreated into his office.

Since Jim Yamada was one of the highest ranking officials at Amsa, Okata wouldn't question anything he'd done.

Joe took his place at the desk at the very front of the office. Everything in Amsa was done according to rank. His seat in the front of the room meant he was the most junior trainee. Tadashi Kamura, at the back, was the most senior.

Joe's problem was that he couldn't keep an eye on the other people in the department when they all sat behind him. He turned on his computer and went to work.

He didn't look up until Mr. Okata's door opened again, and the supervisor inquired icily, "And why are *you* late, Miss Yamada?"

Mariko Yamada breezed through the office. Her long, black hair was swept up in a high ponytail, and she wore a short orange skirt, a white sweatshirt, striped leggings, and lavender sneakers. Joe noted again that Mariko Yamada was very pretty.

And very daring. How did Mariko get away with dressing the way she did? he wondered. Being Jim Yamada's niece probably helped.

"I had to buy roller blades," she explained, flashing her supervisor a dazzling smile. "I want to go skating this weekend."

"Your responsibility was to return to your desk at the end of lunch hour," Mr. Okata said with barely concealed fury.

Mariko shrugged. "You know what, Mr. O? I think you Japanese take work too seriously."

"I will have to discuss this with your uncle," Okata choked out.

The girl shrugged again and sat down at the desk behind Joe's. Joe was torn between admiring her open defiance and wondering whether she was just plain crazy. Japanese people treated one another with respect—at all times. Yet Mariko was deliberately flouting this and every other rule.

Joe supposed there was the possibility that she didn't know how disrespectful she was being. Even though her parents were Japanese, she'd been raised in San Francisco.

He returned to his work and was completely absorbed until Mariko's voice caught his attention. "Tadashi, the question is simple—did you or did you not check the report I wrote yesterday?"

Joe swiveled around to see Mariko standing over Tadashi Kamura's desk.

Kamura peered at his screen, studiously ignoring her—until Mariko pressed the button that switched off his screen. When he looked up, he said, "You are very badly behaved."

"Okata told me to give you my report," Mariko snapped. "I gave it to you, and now I need it back."

Kamura gave an elaborate shrug. "I'm afraid I have more important things to do."

"Fine." Mariko snatched a stack of papers from his desk. "Then I won't bother you." Stuffing the papers into a shopping bag, she headed for the door.

"Wait!" Kamura cried.

Joe realized that Kamura was seriously upset and was tempted to go after Mariko. Mr. Okata was already out of his office, speaking angrily to Kamura, and Joe decided not to risk annoying his supervisor a second time.

Later that afternoon Joe remembered that he, too, had given Kamura a report to check. He had worked on analyzing the specifications of a new camera that was being developed. Joe approached Kamura's desk, bowed, and said in his most polite tone of voice, "Excuse me, Kamura-san, but do you have the report I gave you to check yesterday?"

Kamura grunted, flipped through a pile on his desk, and handed Joe the report.

Surprised, Joe thanked him and returned to his desk. In neat, precise English, Kamura had written a few comments in the margin of the report. The tone of Kamura's comments was condescending, but the criticisms were all valid, all helpful. So why hadn't Kamura done the same for Mariko?

That night after dinner Joe stretched out on the couch in the apartment Mr. Yamada had rented for him and Frank. He still hadn't gotten used to the fact that the typical Japanese workday lasted until at least seven, and he was exhausted.

After a few minutes he perked up enough to tell Frank what had happened that day with Mariko and Kamura. "I'm beginning to wonder if I should add her to my list of suspects," he said.

"Sounds like she's a brat but hardly a suspect," Frank said. "Why do you suspect her?"

"Well, Mariko started working as a trainee a month before the counterfeiting started," Joe said, ticking off his points on his fingers. "She hates being at Amsa. She's smart and does first-rate work, but only when she wants to. She could be the inside person fixing the computer records. Mostly she goes out of her way to bug Mr. Okata."

Frank shook his head. "This counterfeiting is more serious than just bugging someone. These people are out to make a lot of money on the black market. Besides, it would be crazy for the counterfeiter to call attention to herself the way Mariko does. What about Kamura?"

"I'd love him to be our man," Joe said. "He's so obnoxious."

"That's not enough of a reason—" Frank started, but a knock on the door interrupted him.

Joe opened the door and found Mariko Yamada, still carrying the shopping bag with her roller blades and report.

"Hi," she said. "I'm feeling homesick. Do you two want to go see an American movie?"

"Sounds good," Frank said. "What do you want to see?"

Joe held up a hand. "Wait a minute," he broke in. "Before we get into movies, can I ask what was going on in the office today?"

"Oh, you mean between me and Kamura," Mariko said, sounding bored by the whole topic. "The biggest problem between us is that I'm nisei. That means both my parents are Japanese, but I was born and raised in America. According to Kamura, that makes me an inferior human. He thinks it's criminal that I don't speak Japanese. Plus he's not crazy about women and refuses to take anything I do seriously."

That fit in with what Joe knew of Kamura. "What did you take off his desk today?" Joe asked. "He looked as if he were about to have a stroke."

"My report," Mariko replied with a grin. "And"—she reached into her bag and pulled out a computer printout—"the printout beneath it."

Joe was curious. Had Mariko taken the report deliberately? he wondered.

"Maybe you've got my report there," he teased, knowing full well that his report was sitting on his desk.

"No." Mariko held out the printout for a moment, frowning. "That's not what this is."

Joe and Frank had just enough time to see that the printout contained a number of schematics—diagrams for wiring—before Mariko thrust it back into her bag. "Come on," she said, "there's a great vampire movie playing."

With Mariko leading the way, the Hardys set out for the subway.

As they reached the corner a burly young man ran toward them. Instinctively, Joe dodged to the side. Out of the corner of his eye he saw Frank do the same.

Mariko was several paces ahead of them. “Get out of the way!” Joe shouted to her. She wasn’t fast enough, though.

Joe watched in horrified disbelief as the silver blade of a knife flashed out, and Mariko fell to the pavement with a cry.

Chapter Five

WHILE FRANK TOOK OFF after the boy with the knife, Joe knelt beside Mariko. "Are you all right?" he asked, afraid there'd be no answer. He touched the side of her neck with his fingertips and was relieved to feel a strong, even pulse.

Mariko turned her head to him, and Joe felt relief wash through him. Gently he helped her to a sitting position. "Did that guy hurt you?"

Mariko shook her head and swept her long, dark hair back from her face with an angry gesture. "No, he just pushed me."

"You're lucky it wasn't worse. He pulled a knife."

Mariko glanced down at the sidewalk and picked up a thin piece of white twine. "Hey, this was one of the handles on my bag," she said.

"He didn't touch my purse, but he cut away my shopping bag. I can't believe it. That jerk stole my roller blades!"

Joe was just relieved she was okay. Helping her to her feet, he asked, "Did you have anything else in the bag? Of course—your report and the schematic," he said, answering his own question. "Maybe that's what he was after."

Frank returned then, breathing hard and empty-handed. "He got away," he said. "I chased him to the subway station, but he jumped onto a train. Did either of you get a good look at him?"

"I think he was wearing jeans and a T-shirt," Mariko said.

"Definitely," Joe agreed, "and he was built like someone who pumps up."

"Well, that's real specific," Frank said with a sigh. "Come on, we'd better go to the nearest police station and report this."

"Now?" Mariko asked. "We'll miss the movie." Frank's expression changed her mind. "Okay," she added, "we can see the movie *after* the police."

On Saturday at around noon the Journeys tour emerged from the subway to find themselves in Akihabara, Tokyo's bustling electronics district.

"Here," Hiro said, nodding toward the cluttered store windows, "you can find anything and everything that's wired."

"You're not kidding," Margot murmured. "Look at this place—stereos, computers, clocks, vacuum cleaners, washing machines, VCRs, blenders . . ."

What Nancy really wanted to see was the store where Lettie Aldridge had bought her vase. "Are there any stores here that sell ceramics?" she asked Hiro.

"Akihabara's not the best place for that," he answered. "You might want to try Ginza, the shopping district. We're going there tomorrow. Or maybe some of the stores in Kyoto."

Kyoto, Nancy thought. Lettie had mentioned Kyoto, too.

As they walked past yet another window piled high with electronics equipment, something inside caught Nancy's eye. Frank Hardy was standing at the counter, talking to a tall, thin boy who seemed to be about his age.

"Hiro," Nancy said quickly, "I'm going inside this store for a few minutes."

The tour guide nodded. "Fine. We'll meet you at the corner."

Nancy was relieved when no one offered to join her. She was sure Frank was on a case, which meant she couldn't just go up and speak to him.

Entering the store, Nancy carefully walked to a counter across from where Frank was standing and talking to the same guy. "Excuse me," she said to the salesman who came up to her, "I'm interested in buying a computer."

Nancy let the salesman show her several models. Although she didn't glance once at Frank, she was sure he had noticed her.

She wasn't disappointed. After a few minutes Frank and his companion started to leave the store. As they did, Frank brushed by her and slipped a folded piece of paper into her hand. Nancy waited until she was outside again before reading Frank's familiar scrawl:

> Welcome, stranger. Am I ever glad to see you! Can you meet me and Joe tonight for dinner at eight?

The note ended with the name and address of a restaurant.

Nancy smiled, tucked the note in her purse, and rejoined the Journeys group, feeling excited. She'd once been definitely attracted to Frank, but she'd been over that for a while now. Still, there were times when she thought about him.

"Did you buy anything in that store?" Bess asked, detaching herself from Hiro's side.

Nancy shook her head. "I was just looking."

"You?" Bess asked in amazement. "I can see Frank Hardy browsing in an electronics store, not you."

"Actually," Nancy said with a grin, "he was there, checking out the computer games."

Bess's mouth dropped open and she pulled Nancy to one side. "They *are* here and on a case, aren't they?" she whispered.

"I don't know," Nancy answered. "Frank was with someone so I didn't want to let on that I knew him. But we're having dinner with him and Joe at eight—he slipped me a note."

Bess laughed, her blue eyes shining. "Great! I wouldn't miss it for the world."

Joe frowned at the computer screen in front of him. Here it was, a perfectly nice Saturday, and he was at work. In fact, practically everyone at Amsa was working.

Kamura had asked him to run a program on receivers, but what he was actually doing was trying to call up the schematic that Mariko had taken from Kamura's desk. He wished Frank were there. After all, Frank was the boy computer genius.

Frank had told him that the computers in each department were probably linked on a computer network. If he was right, Joe should be able to use his computer to get information stored in Kamura's terminal.

All I have to do is figure out the right set of commands, Joe reminded himself. Frank had given him some suggestions, but so far none of them was working.

"What the—" he sputtered as a list of words in Japanese and English appeared after his last command. He'd called up a list of components for Amsa Elite's new video game cartridge. It was a product that hadn't even hit the market yet.

Joe knew that anything to do with the cartridge was top secret. "Which means," he said to himself, "that I accidentally hit an access code for protected information—exactly the kind of code needed by whoever is counterfeiting Amsa Elite products!"

Joe wasn't sure what to do next. Before he could decide, Mr. Okata interrupted him.

"Mr. Hardy," the supervisor said in ominous tones, "I would like to see you—now."

Mr. Okata wasn't in his usual spot in the doorway of his office. He was standing directly in front of Joe's desk. Joe gulped. "I'll be there in a sec—"

"Immediately!" Mr. Okata ordered.

Joe nodded and followed his supervisor into

his office. Mr. Okata handed Joe a spread sheet he'd turned in the day before and pointed out each and every one of its numerous errors. Joe felt himself turning red as his supervisor droned on and on. "This work is very sloppy," Mr. Okata finally concluded.

"I-I'm sorry," Joe stammered, drawing a complete blank on which form of Japanese apology he should use. "I'll correct the errors at once."

Joe made a slight bow and reflected that the thing probably wouldn't have been such a mess if he hadn't been so distracted trying to solve a case. Unfortunately, that was the last thing in the world he could explain to Mr. Okata.

Joe was eager to save the information on the video game cartridge and couldn't believe what he saw when he sat down. The screen was blank. Someone had tampered with his computer while he had been in Okata's office.

Rapidly, he began punching in various key combinations. Frank had once told him that unless you erased the hard disk, it was almost impossible to actually lose information on a computer. What was easy to do was misplace it, though.

Regardless of what he tried, the screen remained blank. Finally, he just punched in the commands to get to his own work. Still, the screen remained blank.

This was even worse than Joe had thought. Not only was the coded information on the video cartridge gone, so was everything else on his computer!

Someone had just wiped all of his files clean!

Chapter Six

FURIOUS, Joe whirled around to confront everyone in the office. His eyes fell first on Mariko. She had to have witnessed what had happened—unless she was responsible.

"All right," he said to her in a dangerously calm voice. "I want to know—"

Mariko glanced up from her desk, obviously alarmed. She scribbled something on a piece of paper and handed it to Joe.

"Don't say another word," he read to himself in disbelief.

She nodded toward the hallway. Shaking his head, Joe followed Mariko out of the office. That day she was wearing black bicycle shorts, red hightops, and a loose red top with giant black polka dots.

Mariko closed the door behind them. "If something's wrong," she began, "it's very important that you *not* say anything."

"Why shouldn't I—"

"Because you'll lose face," she answered at once. "If there's something wrong with your computer, you have to accept responsibility for it. Otherwise, you'll disgrace yourself in the eyes of everyone in the department."

Joe raked a hand through his hair. "I don't care if they think I'm a talking amoeba," he retorted. "Why should I take the blame for something I didn't do?"

Joe took a deep breath, trying to calm himself. Why was Mariko acting like this? Did it have anything to do with the schematic she took from Kamura the day before? "If you didn't have anything to do with erasing my disk," he said, "why are you telling me to accept the responsibility for it?"

Mariko folded her arms. "Maybe I'm trying to help you. Maybe I don't want Okata thinking all Americans are irresponsible."

"Well, you're not exactly setting a dazzling example yourself," Joe snapped.

Joe calmed himself and decided he wouldn't learn anything by snapping at her. "Tell me," he said, "since when do you care what Okata thinks?"

"I don't have to explain how I feel to you or anyone else."

"Why not? I thought we were friends."

Mariko nodded and smiled. "We are," she said. "That's why I don't want to see you get in trouble. And I don't want Okata thinking all Americans are as—difficult—as I've been.

"So," Mariko went on, "what exactly happened to your computer?"

"Someone erased everything," he told her. "It's all gone—my work, the software programs I was using, even the disk-operating system." Joe didn't mention the game-cartridge data.

If Mariko knew about the data, she gave no indication of it. "Do you have backups?" she asked.

Not of the game-cartridge data, Joe thought. "I've got backup files on most of my work. But not on the systems that run the computer or the software. And there was a lot of software on that thing."

"Someone else in the department will have those programs," Mariko said. "Probably Kamura. You'll just have to load it all again."

"That will take hours," Joe said, groaning.

Mariko shrugged. "Better than blaming someone and having everyone think you're dishonorable."

Joe straightened up, fixing Mariko with a

stony gaze. "Who did it?" he asked her bluntly. "You were there when I was in Okata's office. Who went up to my computer and erased everything?"

"No one," Mariko answered, her eyes on the floor. "No one went near your computer."

"I think this is the place," Nancy said Saturday evening, pointing to a tiny restaurant with a sign in English that read Robatayaki Grill. "Come on, I think I see Joe's blond head in back."

The two girls made their way through the packed restaurant, where the aromas of grilled meat and fish and vegetables filled the air.

"Over here!" cried Joe, jumping up from the table to give both girls a hug. "I probably broke about sixteen rules of Japanese etiquette," he confessed, leading them to the table with his arms still around them.

Frank stood up and gave each girl a hug. "What are you two doing here?" he asked.

"Just vacationing," Bess answered as she sat down.

Frank's dark eyes met Nancy's. "Really?" he asked softly. "*Just* vacationing?"

"Well," Nancy answered with a laugh, "it's mostly a vacation. There's just a little matter of pearl smuggling I'm looking into." She waited until the waiter took their orders before filling the Hardys in on Lettie Aldridge's case.

"Why do the police think the smugglers are operating out of the hotel?" Frank asked.

"I've been wondering about that, too," Nancy said. She hesitated, admiring the delicate arrangement of food on the plate that was being set before her before continuing. "What about you two? I saw Joe wearing a tie the other day, so I *know* you're not on vacation."

Joe grinned, and Frank filled the girls in on the case. "I have a suspect," he finished. "The guy I was with in the electronics store, Isao Matsuda. He works with me in shipping."

"What's suspicious about him?" Bess asked.

"I'm not really sure," Frank answered. "He hasn't done anything weird—it's just that he always acts so nervous. It's as if he's always afraid. It makes me wonder if there's something he's trying to hide."

"I wish I could get something on Kamura," Joe said glumly. He frowned as a piece of grilled chicken dropped through his chopsticks and bounced off his plate onto his lap.

"Smooth move," said Frank. "Really smooth."

Joe retrieved his chicken and grinned at the others. "It was planned," he assured them. "I was merely testing the bounceability of this particular piece of chicken."

"Research and development has fried his brain," Frank explained to Nancy and Bess.

"Did Kamura say anything today about the report that Mariko took?" Nancy asked.

"Not in English," Joe replied. "And he wouldn't talk to Mariko at all. Then again, she wasn't talking to him either."

Nancy noticed that Joe had given up his attempt to use two chopsticks. He was now energetically spearing things with one. "There must be an easier way to eat rice," he murmured.

"Do you really suspect Mariko?" Nancy asked, laughing.

Joe nodded. "It's possible that she saw that game-cartridge data on my screen and erased it."

"She has to be a suspect," Frank said, and poked his brother with his chopstick. "And Joe loves it. It gives him the perfect excuse to get to know her."

Joe gave his brother an irritated look.

"What happened when you went to the police last night?" Nancy asked.

Joe gave a small laugh. "They made a report and then gave us this look that said, 'We have better things to do with our time than chase down stolen roller blades.'" he said.

Nancy finished off her shrimp and vegetable dish. "Did you get a chance to look at the report Mariko took from Kamura's desk?"

"We only got a glimpse of it last night," Frank replied. "It had some wiring diagrams on it. But just about every product Amsa makes has one of those—they're called schematics. I was trying to figure out which product they were for," he said thoughtfully.

"Are all the schematics on file in the research and development department?" Nancy asked.

"Not on my computer," Joe told her. "Maybe on Kamura's. Probably on Mr. Okata's."

"Maybe we can find a way to access the schematics and figure out which one Mariko took from Kamura," Frank said. He became more serious then and stared at Nancy. "You'll let us know if you need any help on your case, won't you?"

Nancy nodded. "I'm glad you two are here."

The four friends exchanged phone numbers and then split up, promising to stay in touch.

Half an hour later Nancy and Bess were back at their hotel, wondering why the police thought the smugglers used this particular hotel.

If they did, how would she prove it? The hotel had over three hundred rooms, plus restaurants, shops, a pool, and special suites for business groups. She couldn't even guess how many people worked there, and it didn't help that the staff spoke only Japanese among themselves.

Even if Nancy overheard something incriminating, she'd never know it.

"Why do you think Hartwell and the Japanese police believe that the smuggling ring is operating out of this hotel?" Nancy asked Bess.

Bess shrugged and opened the door to their room on the twentieth floor. "Maybe Lettie Aldridge wasn't the first mule that the smugglers used."

Nancy stretched out on her bed, considering Bess's answer. "You may be right, but I didn't see anything more about smuggled pearls when I checked the newspapers."

"When did you do that?" Bess asked, amazed.

"When you took that nap this afternoon after we got back from Akihabara. I went over to the public library. I could find only one Tokyo newspaper in English. There was only one article in the last six months that had anything to do with pearls, and it was a report on that theft on the Kii peninsula."

Bess picked up a hairbrush and began brushing out her blond silky curls. "What did it say?"

Nancy sighed, recalling the article. "Thousands of cultured pearls were taken from a pearl farm. Also a few pieces of jewelry that were kept there as samples. The police think the thieves are pretty much untouchable."

"Untouchable?" Bess asked, concentrating on her own reflection in the mirror. "Why? Who are they?"

"The *yakuza,*" Nancy replied grimly. "Japan's criminal underworld."

Chapter Seven

BESS STOOD in the middle of Shinjuku Park the following morning, her head tilted up to gaze at the grove of cherry trees. "This is wonderful," she said. "That scent—I think we're in the loveliest spot in Tokyo."

Nancy had to agree. The hundreds of cherry trees in the garden were laden with blossoms. She walked past a stone lantern and beneath arching branches that formed a canopy of delicate pink flowers. Even the grass was carpeted with pink.

Ahead of her, Gary stopped, bent down, and picked up a sprig of the fragrant flowers.

He winked at her, then dropped to one knee. "The cherry blossoms pale beside your beauty," he intoned theatrically. "And the skies become a mere gray when compared with the blue of your eyes."

"Get up, you lunatic," Nancy said, laughing. "People are staring."

Gary stood up and brushed a dark shock of hair from his eyes. "Let them," he said cheerfully. "Then they'll all know you're one of the prettiest sights in Tokyo."

Nancy blushed. This was getting embarrassing. "I've got to be honest," she told Gary. "I have a boyfriend back home."

"Hey, it's all right. You don't have take this so seriously. There's no pressure. We're going to be traveling together for two weeks. I thought maybe we could be friends and have a good time. Anything wrong with that?" he asked.

"What about Wendy?" Nancy asked. "She seems pretty attached to you."

"Wendy's parents and mine have been friends since before we were born," Gary explained. "We were kind of brought up together. But there's nothing romantic between us."

Nancy wasn't so sure. She'd seen the possessive way Wendy looked at Gary. Then again, Gary did seem to treat Wendy as just a friend.

"So," he said softly, "I repeat my question: Is there anything wrong with our having a good time on this trip?"

Nancy hesitated. "No," she finally told him.

"There's nothing wrong with that—nothing at all."

The next stop on the tour was Ginza, Tokyo's famous shopping district, where Hiro led the group in and out of a series of stores that seemed to sell every imaginable object.

Hiro led them into a tiny store that sold only powders and eyeshadows packaged in beautiful lacquered cases. Nancy, Bess, and Margot each bought eyeshadows. Wendy, who seemed to have an unlimited budget, bought one of nearly every item in the store.

"Good grief!" said Bess after several hours of touring Ginza. "We've seen high-fashion clothes, linen, kites, food, stationery, furniture, paper lanterns. I hate to admit it, but even *I'm* shopped out."

"I know what you mean," Nancy said. "I'm beginning to understand why Lettie Aldridge can't remember which stores she was in during her tour."

"Complaints?" Hiro teased, coming up beside them. He was handsome in his crew neck sweater and jeans. Nancy knew what Bess saw in him.

"Hiro," Nancy said, "I want to bring a vase back for my aunt. Do you know a good place to buy pottery?"

Hiro seemed bewildered by her request.

"All these stores, and you haven't seen any pottery?"

"There was only a store that specialized in dark brown glazes," Nancy said. "But my aunt's living room is blue. I was thinking of something blue and white."

Hiro shrugged. "I'm sure there's someplace in Ginza, but I don't know where."

"Haven't we done enough shopping?" Michael asked, his video camera slung over his shoulder.

"I'm afraid there's one more store on the list. Wendy specially requested that we go there."

"What do they sell?" Margot wanted to know. She was checking the color of the mauve blush against her coffee-colored skin in her compact.

"Pearls," Wendy answered.

Ten minutes later Nancy stared through the glass display case at tray after tray of gleaming pearls—white, pink, cream, blue, gray, and black.

"How much is that one?" Wendy asked, pointing to a double-strand necklace.

The sales clerk took the necklace from the display case and named a price that made Nancy's jaw drop. Even Wendy appeared to be shocked.

"Why are they so expensive?" Bess asked.

"Our pearls take over six years to cultivate,"

the woman answered. "Not only that, but the pearls in this necklace are perfectly matched." She returned the necklace to the case. "Even though these are cultured pearls, grown in oyster beds, they are still considered quite rare. Only one in twenty is fine enough to be sold."

"I had no idea," Michael murmured.

As the sales clerk began to show Wendy some more affordable pieces, Nancy thought about what the woman had said. The pearls that had been hidden in Ms. Aldridge's vase must have been cultured pearls if they came from a pearl farm on the Kii peninsula. Based on the prices she saw here, Nancy guessed that the pearl-smuggling operation had a very high price tag on it. Whoever was involved would go to great lengths to protect themselves.

Nancy didn't get much more time to reflect on the pearls, however. Hiro rushed the group off to purchase box lunches, which they then brought to the *Kabuzika,* the Kabuki theater in Ginza.

"Are you sure it's okay to eat in the middle of a performance?" Nancy asked Hiro.

"You have to," he said. "These plays go on forever. Everyone in the audience would starve to death if they didn't eat during it."

"Fine with me," said Bess, separating her chopsticks.

Wendy sat on Hiro's other side. "I just don't

see how we're going to follow the play if the whole thing is in Japanese," she said.

"Well, you won't follow it word for word," Hiro explained. "But half the fun of Kabuki is the spectacle—you won't need a translation for that."

The performance began and Nancy found that Hiro was right. Even if the play wasn't always understandable, it was always entertaining. There were songs and swordfights, acrobatics and dazzling costumes. She was almost disappointed when two hours later Hiro whispered that the group was leaving.

"Wasn't that incredible?" Margot asked as they left the ornate building.

"Beats the tea ceremony any day," Gary said.

"The actress who played the courtesan was my favorite," said Bess. "She was so beautiful! I mean, I couldn't understand a word she said, but I could tell how much she loved the merchant's son."

Hiro smiled at Bess. "That wasn't an actress playing the courtesan," he told her. "Women have been banned from the Kabuki stage since 1629."

"But—" Bess sputtered. Her eyes widened as she understood what he meant. "You mean the courtesan was played by a *man?*"

"All the women in the play were men," Hiro answered. "In a way, a Kabuki actor is like a pearl. The actor coats himself with layers of makeup and costume and his own skill, until at last he has a surface so beautiful that no one can tell what lies underneath. Just like the pearl that builds up layer upon layer over a grain of sand."

Hiro's words stayed with Nancy. It was not only pearls and Kabuki, she decided. Japanese culture also had a surface so carefully constructed that no one could tell what lay underneath.

Frank leaned back in the kitchen chair, which was slightly too small for him. At six foot one, he was too big for everything in Japan, especially the minuscule apartment he shared with Joe.

He and Joe had spent the day following Isao Matsuda, but they hadn't come up with anything. The thin young man had spent practically the whole day playing soccer. He had played intensely, as if he'd needed to blow off a lot of steam. Frank still had no clue as to what was at the root of the boy's nervousness.

"Do you think that list of components you saw means our counterfeiters are going to counterfeit game cartridges next?" Frank asked Joe.

"Maybe, but not necessarily. It could have just been a file I accessed by mistake."

Frank stood up and stretched. "Mr. Yamada called while you were out getting these," he said, nodding to the rice cakes. "The latest reports show that the number of counterfeit CD players arriving in the U.S. has dropped over the last two months. So maybe that means the counterfeiters are gearing up to counterfeit a new product."

"Like the video game cartridge," Joe guessed.

"You got it. I'd really like to see that list of components," said Frank. "You still don't remember the command you used?"

Joe shook his head.

"What about Mariko?" Frank asked.

Joe grinned. "I asked her out. We're going to a club tonight."

Frank couldn't believe what he was hearing. "Terrific," he said. "You think she may have erased all your computer files, and you start dating. What will you do if she turns out to be the counterfeiter—marry her?"

"Very funny," Joe said. "Anyway, we don't know who erased my disk."

"Mariko's being very mysterious about that schematic she took from Kamura, and she wouldn't tell you who *did* erase your drive," Frank reminded his brother. "So let's say, for argument's sake, that she did erase it."

He held up a hand to stop Joe's objection. "The question is, why?" Frank went on. "It must be because that top secret game-cartridge information shouldn't have been accessible, so when you did access it, someone had to make sure you couldn't call it up again." He smacked his hand down on the tabletop. "We're definitely onto something, and someone is definitely trying to stop us."

"I'm still going out with her," Joe replied evenly. "You want to come?"

Shaking his head, Frank said, "No, I want to try to figure out how to find that data again. If it was on your disk, it's gone from there for good. But I think you tapped into a network that links your computer to others in the company. If the data is in a net, we should be able to retrieve it again."

"Even if it's protected by a code?"

Frank grinned. "Didn't you ever hear that old saying? Codes are like rules. They're meant to be broken."

"So where did Hiro take you for dinner?" Nancy asked a dreamy-eyed Bess later that Sunday.

"Just a little noodle shop," Bess said. "But the food was delicious. And guess what! Hiro has tonight free, so he's taking us to Downtown L.A."

Nancy frowned. "Los Angeles? Aren't we on the wrong continent for going to L.A.?"

"Not *that* L.A.," Bess said, laughing. "This one is a club in the Roppongi district—Hiro says it's the hottest one in Tokyo." She held out a small rectangular wooden box. "Look what he gave me."

Nancy opened the box and saw two black lacquered sticks, each topped with two little knobs. "Are these—"

"Hairpins," Bess finished for her with a giggle.

"Are you going to wear them tonight?" Nancy asked.

"In a place called Downtown L.A.? No way!" Bess put an arm around Nancy's shoulder. "Tonight I dress pure rock 'n' roll."

An hour later Hiro ushered Nancy and Bess into Downtown L.A. They really had dressed for dancing. Bess was wearing a short suede skirt, boots, and an oversize vest and T-shirt. Nancy wore a close-fitting green minidress with rhinestone earrings, and Hiro had on a black silk button-down shirt and black jeans.

The threesome paused inside the door to look around. The space was huge, a series of cavernous rooms connected by exposed metal staircases and catwalks. It was packed with people dancing to a driving beat.

"Check out the balcony," Bess shouted over the music.

Nancy immediately spotted Joe Hardy. He was sitting at a cramped table with a pretty girl who had long, black hair.

"Let's grab a table," Hiro suggested, moving toward the stairway.

"Why don't you let me do that?" Nancy offered quickly.

Bess caught her cue at once. Pulling Hiro onto the dance floor, she said, "Come on, let's dance."

Nancy wound her way up the crowded staircase, glancing at the crowd. She chose a table not far from Joe's and sat down.

A few seconds later Joe appeared at her table, his date at his side. Nancy wondered if she was the suspect he'd mentioned.

"Mind if we join you?" Joe asked.

Nancy smiled. "I was hoping you would."

"Nancy, this is Mariko Yamada," Joe said. "Mariko's another Amsa trainee, and Nancy's—"

"An old friend," Nancy supplied. She smiled at Mariko, but the other girl regarded her with a cool, blank expression.

Nancy scanned the crowd below. "Is Frank here?"

"No, he's being boring tonight," Joe replied. "He's home doing some research. You know Frank. He has to be super-trainee."

"Are you also in a trainee program?" Mariko asked Nancy politely.

"No, my friend Bess and I are here on a tour," Nancy replied.

Mariko brushed a glossy strand of hair out of her eyes. "You're lucky," she said.

"We're here for only two weeks," Nancy said. "It doesn't seem nearly enough time to really get to know this country."

Mariko's dark eyes narrowed. "Sometimes you wind up knowing more than you want to."

"Not me," Joe put in. "I'm incredibly nosy. For example, isn't that guy down there by the bar another Amsa trainee? He looks familiar."

Following Joe's gaze, Nancy saw the guy who had been in the electronics store with Frank. He was talking to a slim, fine-featured man in his twenties wearing an elegant tan suit and sunglasses.

"That's Isao Matsuda," Mariko said. "He works in shipping. He's the one who always gets winded in the morning calisthenics class."

Joe stood up. "Hey, I'm going to invite him to join us. And his friend, too."

He hadn't gone two steps before Mariko pulled him back. "Are you crazy?" she demanded. "Don't you see who he's with?"

Joe shrugged. "The best-dressed guy in Japan?"

"Look at his hand," Mariko said fiercely, "his right hand."

The man in the suit was holding a glass in his right hand. Nancy saw that the tip of his littlest finger was missing.

"That was no accident," Mariko said. "In the *yakuza*—Japan's equivalent of the mob—it's a traditional punishment. If a member of the *yakuza* dishonors himself or the others, he's required to chop off the tip of a finger to show atonement."

"That's gross," said Joe, grimacing.

No wonder Isao looked scared, Nancy thought. He's linked to the criminal underworld. The newspaper had said that the *yakuza* were probably behind the theft of the pearls.

Nancy eyed Isao Matsuda with new curiosity. If a *yakuza* was behind the pearl smuggling, *and* a *yakuza* was talking to one of Frank and Joe's suspects, then maybe the two cases were linked!

Chapter Eight

NANCY'S EYES MET JOE'S. She knew he'd picked up on Isao Matsuda's *yakuza* connection. In the next instant his face took on a look of nonchalance.

As Bess and Hiro approached their table, Joe took Mariko's hand. "Want to dance?" She nodded, and the two of them left for the dance floor.

"You've found friends in Tokyo already?" Hiro asked as he and Bess joined Nancy at the table.

"Joe's an old friend," Nancy explained. "I never expected to run into him here in Tokyo." He definitely seemed to be falling for Mariko—not that that should have surprised Nancy. Joe fell in love nearly as often as Bess.

"Do you want to dance?" Hiro asked Nancy.

"Thanks—maybe in a bit," she said, standing up to peer over the banister. "Right now it's fun just watching."

"Boy, that's one weird dance Joe's doing," Bess said as Hiro came to stand beside her. "He's actually sashaying Mariko across the floor."

"It's probably culture shock," Nancy murmured. Actually, she knew exactly what Joe was doing, but she couldn't say anything to Bess in front of Hiro.

Joe was actually heading straight for Isao Matsuda. The *yakuza* was gone, but Isao still stood at the bar, restlessly sliding his glass from one hand to the other. Joe and Mariko were almost to the bar when Isao saw them and bolted.

Nancy watched the scene, fascinated. Was Isao afraid to be seen by Joe and Mariko? Did he even know Joe? Or was there another reason he'd run?

Nancy scanned the crowd, searching for Isao or the *yakuza*. Both were gone.

"Is something wrong?" Hiro asked.

Bess gave him a dazzling smile. "Just watching the floor show," she answered lightly.

And wondering what it all means, Nancy added to herself.

* * *

Nancy was wakened Monday morning by a knock on the hotel room door. "What time is it?" she mumbled groggily, rubbing her eyes.

Bess peered at the travel alarm on the nightstand between their beds. "Seven A.M.," she reported. "It feels like five."

"That's because we didn't get to sleep until two," Nancy said.

The knock sounded again.

"Make them go away," Bess grumbled.

Nancy sat up and put on her robe. "It won't do any good," she said. "We have to join the group at eight, and we've got to eat breakfast first."

She went to the door and opened it. No one was there. It took a moment for Nancy to understand who had knocked. "I take it back," she said. "Breakfast just found us."

Stooping down, she lifted a tray from the floor. "Mmmm," she said, peering under the lid of one of the dishes. "Omelettes, hash browns, and biscuits. Plus a pot of coffee. And a vase with cherry blossoms."

Nancy opened the small envelope that was propped up against the base of the vase. "'Dear Nancy,'" she read aloud. "'Journeys gives us a free afternoon today. How about spending it with me? Hope you and Bess enjoy breakfast—Gary.'"

Bess looked at Nancy mischievously. "Well, are you going to?"

"Going to what?"

"Spend the afternoon with him, of course."

Nancy hesitated. "I don't know," she said. "I should talk to Lettie Aldridge again or try—"

The phone rang then, and Nancy picked it up. A few moments later she hung up. "We just got another invitation for this afternoon. That was Frank. He and some of the Amsa trainees are going out to the sumo stables to watch an exhibition sumo match. Want to go?"

Bess looked doubtful. "You mean, wrestling?"

Nancy nodded. "Isao Matsuda is going to be there."

"Then I guess we're going. But Gary's going to be disappointed."

"Not necessarily," Nancy said. "Frank said it's okay to bring friends. I'll invite Gary." Glimpsing the smile that lifted the corners of Bess's mouth, Nancy added, "And something tells me you'll invite Hiro."

Finally! Frank thought to himself as he and Isao Matsuda crossed the skywalk that connected Amsa headquarters with the smallest of the Amsa warehouses.

Frank had been waiting for a chance to get into this warehouse. It was the one where the

Amsa Elite line was stored just before being shipped abroad.

Early that morning Frank's supervisor had dumped a box filled with shipping records on his desk and sent him and Isao to try to straighten out a mix-up.

Isao. His meeting Sunday night with the *yakuza* had propelled him to the top of Frank's suspect list.

Isao showed their clearance papers to a guard. The two boys were ushered into an elevator and then led into a room the size of an airplane hangar. Shipping cartons were stacked floor to ceiling. Three narrow aisles provided the only floor space that wasn't covered with cartons.

"So," Isao said, setting his own box of shipping documents on the floor. "We have orders here from all our American distributors. Mr. Hamaguchi says there's been some mix-up in deliveries."

"What kind of mix-up?" Frank asked, instantly alert. Maybe the mix-up was related to the counterfeiting.

Isao shrugged. "He didn't say. But the third aisle is outgoing orders. We have to check them against these shipping forms and make sure everything matches."

"That could take days."

Isao nodded. "Better start."

The two boys worked silently. At first Frank examined each carton and document eagerly, sure he'd find some clue to the counterfeiters. But everything matched up. Perfectly.

"Let's take a break," he said when they'd been at it two hours. "I'm going to be seeing routing slips in my dreams."

Isao nodded stiffly and sat down on one of the cartons.

"You're going to the sumo stables today, right?" Frank asked. He already knew that Isao was going, but he couldn't think of any other way to start a conversation.

Isao nodded.

"What are they like?" Frank asked. "I mean, have you been there before?"

"No, but I've seen pictures. The stables have sumo rings, a training hall, dorms for the wrestlers, a big kitchen where they all eat." Isao shrugged. "Not much else."

"How come you've never gone to see them before?"

Isao gave Frank one of his rare smiles. "I lived on Kyushu before coming to Tokyo for the trainee program. It's a quiet island. No sumo stables there. And since I've been at Amsa, I haven't had much free time." Isao stood up and stretched. "We'd better get back to work."

Frank considered Isao again. Was he in on the counterfeiting? Maybe it was time for a few innocent questions. "I'd sure like to have one of these for my own," he said, pointing to a carton of CD players.

"There's a company discount," Isao told him.

"I couldn't afford it even with the discount," Frank admitted. "Not unless I got one real cheap."

"Then you don't want an Amsa Elite. There are plenty of good, affordable CD players around. That store we were in the other day sells them."

"Yeah, but I really want one of these," Frank persisted.

Isao gave a gruff nod. "Better start saving your money."

Well, Frank thought, at least Isao hadn't offered to sell him one. He almost wished he had; it would have confirmed that Isao was mixed up in something illegal.

The counterfeits couldn't be in Amsa warehouses unless someone in shipping was involved, Frank reminded himself. If it wasn't Isao, who was it? Their supervisor, Mr. Hamaguchi?

At three o'clock Isao called a halt. "We'd better leave if we're going to get to the stables," he said. "I still can't believe Hamaguchi is giving us time off. We're lucky sumo's his favorite sport."

Frank put down the carton of video game

cartridges he was checking. "What's that?" he asked, looking at Isao's clipboard.

"A carbon of an address label," Isao replied.

"But it has two addresses on it," Frank said. The second was for an American distributor, but the first was a Tokyo street number. Frank memorized the address.

"Must be an error," Isao said, crossing out the Tokyo address.

"Must be," Frank said, hoping it was what he was looking for.

Nancy, Bess, Gary, Hiro, Frank, and a group of shipping department trainees had met outside Amsa headquarters and ridden out to the stables together. The trip had been fun.

"You're in the heart of sumo land here," Hiro said. "There are several stables nearby."

"Why are they called stables?" Bess asked.

"Because the wrestlers *are* owned by the owner of a stable, the way racehorses are."

"You're kidding," Gary said. "No free agents?"

"It's not baseball," Hiro explained with a wry smile. "To become a sumo wrestler, you're recruited into a stable before your thirteenth birthday. The rules are very strict in a sumo stable. Apprentices act as servants for the senior wrestlers. They do all the chores and cooking in addition to their own training and schoolwork. In fact, when wrestlers retire, they usually get jobs as chefs."

"It must be Food Heaven," Bess said. "Can you imagine being told to eat as much as you want all the time? I guess it's fun but not too healthy."

"Don't be fooled," Hiro said. "Under all that fat is tremendous muscle."

Gary winked at Nancy. "Didn't you tell me you came to Japan for the sumo wrestling?"

"I did, didn't I?" Nancy said, surprised that he remembered her joking around that first day.

"I think it's going to be pretty comic," Gary predicted as they entered the sumo stable. "Watching big, fat guys wearing next to nothing, pushing each other around."

"Oh, look!" Bess said softly.

In front of them a single line of sumo wrestlers filed into the building. Nancy had never seen anything quite like their solemn procession. The wrestlers were even bigger than she'd imagined. Dressed in formal black kimonos and wooden clogs, their hair in traditional top knots, they had the most regal bearing she'd ever seen.

Beside her, Gary shook his head. "Maybe *comic* wasn't the right adjective."

"I think *awesome* is better," Frank said.

Although the match they were about to see was only an exhibition match, the arena was crowded with spectators, and the group had to split up. Nancy wound up sitting with Hiro, Bess, and Gary. Frank and Isao sat on the other side of the ring with a few other trainees. Another group of trainees sat behind Nancy.

The first two wrestlers entered the ring and began the prefight rituals. First they stretched out.

"Look how limber they are!" Bess exclaimed. "They're in full splits with their chests touching the floor."

"Now what are they doing?" Gary asked as both wrestlers stamped hard on the ground and stretched one leg sideways.

"That's ritual, not warm-up," Hiro explained. "They're driving the evil spirits from the ring. And now they're purifying the air," he said as both men began to toss salt into the air. "The rules are simple. The first wrestler to push the other out of the ring or make him touch the ground with any part of his body other than the soles of his feet wins."

With the opening ceremonies complete, the two wrestlers assumed the half-squatting starting positions. They stared for a moment, as if gauging each other. Then one burst forward, and the wrestling began.

With Hiro supplying a running commentary, Nancy found sumo wrestling totally absorbing. Between matches she checked to see if Frank was enjoying the matches as much as she was.

Frank wasn't in his seat. She quickly spotted him walking swiftly toward the exit. Just ahead of him was Isao Matsuda.

Frank secretly followed Isao out of the arena and across the grounds toward the back of the compound. Dusk was gathering, and in the dim light the grounds seemed deserted.

As Isao reached the very last building in the compound, a single figure emerged from a doorway. He seemed to be about eighteen and was dressed in sweats with his long hair hanging loose. Frank guessed that the guy was one of the apprentice wrestlers.

Frank sneaked up on the two, hidden by the pine trees surrounding the buildings. Isao said he'd never been here before, and yet he went straight to this building without hesitation. *And* he knew one of the wrestlers.

Isao reached into his jacket, took out a small paper bag, and handed it to the wrestler. The wrestler handed Isao an envelope.

What was being exchanged here? Frank wondered. He stepped a little closer.

Suddenly the wrestler turned in Frank's direction, and with no warning he rushed Frank.

Frank spun and took off, but he didn't get very far. Massive hands clamped down around his waist. The next thing Frank knew, his feet left the ground and he was flying through the air.

Chapter Nine

NANCY GLANCED at her watch and frowned. Frank and Isao had left the arena more than twenty minutes ago. Isao had just returned, but there was no sign of Frank. Nancy had an uneasy feeling that something was wrong.

"Where are you going?" Gary asked as she stood up. "The match isn't over yet."

"Um—I have to use the restroom," Nancy lied. "I'll be right back."

Nancy quickly checked the corridors off the wrestling hall. Frank wasn't in sight, so she stepped outside. She was surprised to see that dusk had fallen. Compared to the raucous cheers of the arena, the rest of the compound was silent. The sky was a deep, calm blue. In the distance she heard the delicate chime of a wind bell.

Cautiously Nancy began to make her way across the grounds. It was nearly dark when she reached the back of the compound—and all but stumbled over a body lying on the ground. She knelt beside it, her heart racing. "Frank?"

"Nan?" With difficulty, he rolled onto his side to face her.

"What happened?" Nancy asked, checking for signs of injury. "Are you all right?"

"I'm fine," Frank said, "for someone who was just thrown twenty-five feet." He shook his head. "And they say humans can't fly."

"You *are* all right," Nancy said, smiling in spite of her worry. "Now will you please tell me what you're talking about?"

Frank pulled himself up to a sitting position. "I followed our friend Isao out of the arena. He had a rendezvous with a wrestler," Frank explained. "A guy who was too young to be one of the pros, but he was definitely sumo."

"And?" Nancy prompted.

"Matsuda handed him a small paper bag in exchange for a plain white envelope."

"Money?"

"That's what I'm guessing."

Sitting back on her heels, Nancy asked. "Then what?"

Frank grimaced. "Then I got this insane idea to get a closer look. They must have heard me."

"Bad move?" Nancy guessed.

"That's the understatement of the year. The wrestler literally tossed me out of the way. I mean, for a while there I was totally airborne." Frank rubbed his head ruefully. "By the time I could move again, they were both gone and you were here. Great detective work, huh?"

Nancy leaned back against one of the pine trees, thinking. This was the first chance she and Frank had had to talk since she saw Isao at the club the night before. "So far we know Isao is connected to at least one member of the *yakuza,*" she said. "And we know the *yakuza* were probably behind the original theft of the pearls. Now Isao is conducting secret meetings with a sumo wrestler."

"There's something else, too," said Frank. "All of the other junior wrestlers were at the match. I got the feeling that it's the sort of event they don't dare miss. It made me wonder if that sumo wrestler was—I don't know—in disgrace or something."

Nancy nodded. "Let's say Isao is selling something. The question is, was he selling pearls or counterfeit electronics? Do you still think he's connected to Amsa's counterfeiting?"

Frank shrugged. "We worked together this afternoon. I fished around a little and didn't get anything. But then he lied to me. He told me he'd never been here before, and he obviously has."

Nancy shook her head. "That's not enough to link him to the Amsa deal unless the *yakuza* are behind the counterfeiting *as well* as the pearls."

"The *yakuza* are behind a lot of things," Frank said thoughtfully. "There are different groups of *yakuza*, the way there are different gangs in the States. It's not like they're all guilty of all crimes."

Nancy stood up, feeling restless. "We're not getting anywhere," she said. "We need something more solid."

"Like a lead," Frank agreed. Using a pine tree for support, he got to his feet. "The only thing I'm sure of is that Isao is involved in something out of the ordinary. I'm going to keep an eye on him."

Gingerly he began to walk back to the arena. "And," he concluded, "I'm definitely going to avoid his friends from now on."

"I can't believe Frank got into a fight with a sumo wrestler," Bess said as she washed off her makeup that night.

"I don't think it was much of a fight," Nancy said. "But it's one more thing about Isao that doesn't add up. I'm wondering if he isn't a suspect in both our cases." She slumped down in the hotel room chair. "Actually he's our *only* suspect in the pearl case. I haven't even gotten close to figuring out who's behind the smuggling!"

Nancy reached for her purse and took out the piece of broken vase she'd been carrying since her first day in Tokyo. "I've got to find other vases like this one," she said. "It's the only real clue we have. Somewhere in Tokyo or Kyoto there's got to be a store that sells them. Then, hopefully, the store will lead us to the counterfeiters."

"You said you wanted to check out the seniors' tour, too," Bess reminded her. "Did you talk to the Olsons?"

"I caught them this morning," Nancy replied. "We only had about two seconds before Kenji hurried them off, but they told me they hadn't seen any pottery like this. What I need to find out is if they're scheduled to go someplace that our tour doesn't go. I'll have to get to them early tomorrow." She stood up and gave a luxurious stretch. "But now I'm going to take a hot bath."

Bess smiled at the sound of a sharp rap on the door. "Who do you think it is this time? More room service, courtesy of Gary?"

Nancy shrugged and went to the door. "Who is it?" she called.

"Please," said a trembling voice. "Let me in! I mustn't be caught in the hall!"

"Lettie?" Nancy said, opening the door.

It was indeed Lettie Aldridge, who stood dressed in slippers and a pink terry cloth robe. She seemed frail, but there was a spark in her eyes that hadn't been there earlier.

"Come in," Nancy said quickly. "Have a seat. Is everything all right?"

"I sneaked out of my room!" Lettie said, obviously pleased with herself. "I just couldn't stand another second of being cooped up! The police told me that I might be allowed to go home tomorrow, but in the meantime I was to remain where I was."

"That's wonderful!" Nancy said. "If they're going to let you go, it means they're convinced you're not mixed up in the smuggling."

"They'd have to be extremely stupid to believe I was," the elderly woman said with a sniff. "I wanted to thank you girls for being so nice, and I wanted to tell you that I've been doing a little sleuthing on my own."

Nancy couldn't hide her surprise. "You have?"

"This is the third time today I've been out of my room," Lettie informed them proudly.

"Lettie," Nancy said worriedly, "you really shouldn't risk antagonizing the police."

"I'm the one who's a suspect," Lettie said. "I had to do something to help myself. So I did."

Lettie placed both hands on her knees and

leaned forward. "I was on the fifth floor—or was it the sixth? Anyway, I saw one of the maids open a linen closet, only there wasn't linen inside. The closet was filled with vases—just like mine."

"Are you sure?" Bess asked.

"I'm not certain about the floor," Lettie admitted. "But I know I saw a linen closet that was filled with those vases. Shelves of them!"

"Have you told the police about this?" Nancy asked. "You definitely should, you know."

"I don't care for either the Tokyo police or Mr. Hartwell. I see no reason to make their jobs easier."

"It might help us stop the pearl smugglers," Nancy said gently. "Look, I'll try to check out the linen closet tomorrow. We'll see you back to your room," she offered.

Nancy and Bess escorted Ms. Aldridge back to her room and said their goodbyes. Then Nancy and Bess returned to their own floor. They'd just gotten out of the elevator when they saw Hiro coming toward them. Bess's face lit up with pure happiness.

"Where have you two been?" he asked in a teasing tone. His eyes lingered on Bess in a way that made Nancy sure the crush was mutual.

"We said goodbye to Ms. Aldridge," Bess answered. "The police may let her go home tomorrow."

Hiro smiled. "I know," he said. "The police contacted Journeys. We're all grateful they're letting her go. The last few days have been hard on her. She's a very brave woman."

"That's for sure," Nancy agreed. "We had quite a talk."

"Oh? What did you talk about?" Hiro asked curiously.

"What else?" Bess answered blithely. "Pearls."

Chapter Ten

NANCY WAS UP and dressed well before breakfast the next morning. Bess was still in the shower, so Nancy scrawled a quick note to her and left the room.

She got out of the elevator on the sixth floor and fingered the thin piece of metal in her pocket. Her eyes checked every door, taking note of each one that didn't have a room number.

Nancy circled back to the elevator and sat on the nearby bench for a moment, mentally reviewing what she'd seen.

Altogether there were four potential linen closets and probably four more just like them on the fifth floor. Nancy didn't like to have to pick one lock, let alone eight. It would have helped if Lettie had remembered on which floor she had seen the vases. But since she hadn't . . .

Nancy made her way to the first unmarked door and took out her lock-picking set. I hope this thing works on Japanese doors, she thought. Her heart pounded as she inserted the thin piece of metal and turned it to the right, then to the left. A moment later the door swung open.

No vases there—only linen. With a sigh, she moved to the next closet.

The contents of the second linen closet were identical to those of the first. But when Nancy stepped inside the third and turned on her flashlight, she found the shelves empty—except for something on the floor near the back.

Nancy stooped down and slid her hand under the bottom shelf and drew out a shard of blue-and-white ceramic. The glaze was identical to the piece in her purse.

The vases had been in there! They'd obviously been moved. Nancy knew she ought to go to Hartwell, but she wasn't sure how to explain breaking into the hotel's linen closets. She'd simply have to tell him what Lettie saw, but first she had to wait until Lettie was safely on her way home. She wouldn't risk getting the woman in more trouble.

Nancy took the elevator to the hotel lobby

and hoped she could find the Olsons before they left for the day.

She found them in the coffee shop, seated at a table with Bess. "Mind if I join you?" Nancy asked.

"Delighted," John Olson said.

"Could I ask you something?" Nancy said after a waitress stopped and took her order for pancakes and orange juice. "When you decided to visit Japan, what made you choose the Journeys tour?"

"The price and the itinerary," Mr. Olson said at once. "They offer a great package."

If the Journeys organization was somehow involved in the smuggling, it would make sense that they'd offer special incentives to seniors in order to draw more unsuspecting couriers.

Adele Olson winked at her. "Bess tells us your group has the best guide in Tokyo."

"It looks that way," Nancy said with a laugh. "Hiro's been great. Who's with your group?"

"Most of the time a boy named Kenji," Mrs. Olson answered. "He's very good except he tells us the bloodiest stories about every site we visit."

Mr. Olson set down his coffee cup. "History is bloody, Adele," he said patiently.

Nancy had the feeling that this was an old argument between them. "Has your tour gone to Kyoto yet?" she asked, changing the subject.

"We're going tomorrow, as a matter of fact," Mrs. Olson said.

"We're not scheduled to go until next week," Bess put in, eating her omelette.

"Would you do me a favor when you're there tomorrow?" Nancy asked.

"Of course," Mr. Olson said.

"I'd like to find a vase like this," she said, pulling out the blue-and-white fragment. "If I give you money and you see a vase in this pattern, could you—"

"We'd be glad to," Mrs. Olson told her.

Mr. Olson studied the shard for a moment. "We'll do what we can, but now I believe we've got to join the rest of our tour."

"Why didn't you tell them the truth?" Bess asked abruptly. "Why did you give them that whole song and dance about your aunt?"

"Because if they do walk into that shop, I want them to look completely innocent," Nancy answered. "If they act as if they know what's going on, they could be in danger— Bess, I just got an idea. What if you and I take an overnight trip to Kyoto tomorrow?"

"Tomorrow?" Bess echoed in dismay. "We're only here for two weeks, and I'm having such a great time with Hiro . . ."

Nancy felt bad about pressuring Bess. Knowing how crazy she was about Hiro, it wasn't fair to ask her to make a choice. "It's okay," Nancy said quickly. "You stay. I'll go to Kyoto on my own."

"Can you give me some time to think it over?" Bess asked quietly.

"Bess, you don't have to—"

"I'll let you know," Bess said. Before Nancy could argue further, Bess got up and brought her check to the cashier.

Nancy finished her breakfast, thinking about Bess. She and Bess had traveled together so many times that she just assumed her friend would want to go with her. I guess things are changing, Nancy thought as she wandered into the lobby.

Bess stood by a pillar, talking with Hiro. A little later she walked up to Nancy, smiling. "It's all settled," she announced.

"What is?" Nancy asked, mystified.

"We're going to Kyoto tomorrow, and we're staying in a beautiful *ryokan*—you know, one of those old, traditional inns. Hiro's arranging it for us."

Nancy blinked. "I think I missed something here. What made you change your mind?"

"Hiro," Bess said, grinning. "He said he thought I'd love Kyoto, and that we should definitely go."

"Why do we have to do this during lunch hour?" Joe asked Frank as they left Amsa's headquarters Tuesday at noon. "I happen to be starving. Can't we check out this address after work?"

"No," Frank mumbled. "We'd never find it at night. We have to go *now.*" He unfolded a map.

"Give me that," said Joe, reaching for the map and hailing a cab.

"I don't see the street on this map," Joe said inside the cab.

Frank gave the driver the address, then turned to his brother. "It may not be on the map," he said. "Yesterday Hiro was telling us that when Tokyo was rebuilt after World War Two, it was rebuilt as a bunch of tiny little centers, almost like villages. All the villagers knew the way around their own streets, so they didn't bother to name half of them. Also, they numbered the houses according to the order in which they'd been built. So number forty-six could be next to number nine."

"Great," said Joe. "It'll take us the rest of the day to find this place. Mr. Okata will have a coronary. I already spend half my time apologizing to him, not to mention—"

Frank tuned out Joe's grumbling. He wasn't sure how he was going to explain his absence to his supervisor, Mr. Hamaguchi, either. Worst of all, he wasn't sure the address wasn't some sort of wild-goose chase. What if they came away empty-handed?

"Frank." Joe's voice was a low growl.

"What?"

"This cab hasn't moved for ten minutes. In case you haven't noticed, we're in a primo traffic jam."

"How close are we to this address?" Frank asked the driver.

The driver shrugged. "One kilometer, maybe two."

"Then we walk," Joe said.

Frank nodded, paid the driver a ridiculous amount of money, and got out of the cab. "Now what?"

Joe pointed toward a nearby *koban,* one of Tokyo's many police substations. "We ask an officer."

Twenty minutes later the Hardys arrived at what looked like an abandoned office building. It was only three stories tall, built of concrete. Most of the windows were boarded up, and the blackened walls made Frank wonder if a fire hadn't swept through it at some point.

"This doesn't look like a legitimate warehouse," he observed.

Joe pointed to a heavy padlock on the front door. "Someone's taking trouble to keep it locked, though. There must be a reason they don't want visitors."

He wandered around to the side of the building. "Over here," he called to Frank. Joe pointed to a first-floor window that had been boarded up. "The plywood's split. I think we can get in."

Frank went first, wedging open the split in the wood. "I hope the Japanese are cool about trespassing," he whispered to himself in the darkened room.

Frank stood motionless, listening for noises and giving his eyes a minute to adjust to the darkness. "I think it's just you and me," he whispered as his brother joined him. "This was definitely an office building." He pointed to wall partitions and a broken desk that lay in the center of the floor.

Slowly the Hardys checked out the abandoned building. They found more broken and charred furniture on the first floor and an elevator that didn't work. Cobwebs covered everything.

Joe headed for the dust-covered stairwell and slowly began to work his way up. Frank pointed ahead of them, and Joe turned around, his eyes wide. "Footprints!" he whispered.

"Careful," Frank whispered back. "We may not be the only ones here."

The second floor was much like the first—

abandoned offices and scattered, wrecked furniture. Joe nodded to the stairwell, which continued upward. "Shall we?" he said with exaggerated politeness.

Frank took the lead this time. Amazingly the building seemed to have gotten quieter. He found himself holding his breath as he reached the top of the stairs and gently pushed open the landing door.

"Bingo," he said.

The room was filled with cardboard cartons, all of them new. His adrenaline racing, Frank walked over to the closest box. The top was open. He took out a pocket flashlight and shone it inside. "Tape reels," he said. "The kind that would fit in a videocassette. And here's the circuitry. These are all unmarked. I don't see the Amsa Elite symbol. These could be the counterfeit components."

Joe was peering at a stack of open boxes at the far end of the room. "I bet the Amsa Elite stuff is over there. Those look like they might be video game cartridges."

"Excellent!" Frank said softly. "We've got the proof we need." He began to cross the room to check out the cartridges, but Joe's voice stopped him.

"Frank." Joe's voice had taken on an urgency. "We've got company."

Frank whirled around. Standing in the doorway was a muscular young man. Frank recognized him immediately—it was the guy who'd stolen Mariko's bag! In his hands was a long, wooden pole, and he was swinging it with the practiced grace of someone who knew how to kill with it.

Chapter Eleven

JOE TENSED, staring at the man with the long wooden staff. He knew it was only a matter of seconds before the attack began.

"That's a *bo,*" Frank whispered to him, identifying the traditional Okinawan weapon.

It figured that Frank would use a time like this to give a martial arts lesson. "I know that," Joe whispered back. "You're not the only one who's studied karate, you know. What are we going to do?"

If the man understood English, he gave no sign of it. He advanced on them slowly, the *bo* cutting through the air in swift, powerful arcs.

"There are two of us and one of him," Frank pointed out. "Do you want to keep that jacket you're wearing?"

Joe immediately understood what Frank meant. "Not particularly," he said, slipping it off.

"Then do me a favor and do something useful with it," Frank said, walking toward their attacker.

"I'll give it some thought," Joe promised.

Without warning, the man thrust the *bo* forward, aiming it at Frank's stomach. Frank sidestepped quickly. The man swung again, and Frank jumped backward. Joe winced as the *bo* smashed into one of the boxes just beyond his brother. As the third swing came toward him, Frank stepped forward and grabbed the staff, wrenching it from his opponent's hands. "Now!" he shouted.

Joe was already in motion. He hurled his jacket over the man's head and brought him to the ground.

"Hold him," Frank ordered. "Now let's try to get some answers."

Joe knelt on top of their captive, pinning his arms to the ground, but the man didn't stop fighting. He was struggling wildly. Frank knelt beside Joe and helped hold down their attacker.

"Who are you?" Joe demanded. "Why did you steal Mariko's bag?"

The man didn't answer. From the lack of response in his eyes Joe guessed he didn't understand English. He tried one more time, "What's going on in this warehouse?"

Their captive's eyes dulled, and his body went still. Reflexively, the brothers relaxed their hold.

In that second the man broke away from them with a frightening burst of energy, throwing Joe backward to the floor. When Joe righted himself, the man was already across the room, where the *bo* lay. He picked up the staff and screamed something. Joe didn't know the words, but he definitely understood their general meaning.

This man was going to kill them.

"Let's get out of here!" Frank shouted.

Joe needed no further encouragement. He and Frank raced down the stairs, aware of their attacker following close behind.

Joe reached the ground floor first, launched himself through the opening in the window, and pulled Frank through after him. Once on the street they kept running. They finally slowed down when they were about ten blocks from the warehouse. "Is he still following us?" Joe asked, panting.

"I don't think so," Frank said. He bent over and rested his hands on his knees, breathing hard. "But I don't want to hang around to find out."

Joe glanced at his watch, and his face

blanched. "Frank, we just took a two-hour lunch. By the time we get back through traffic, it'll be nearly three hours. I can't go back and face Okata—especially without a jacket. Will you tell him I'm sick?"

Frank said, "Do you know how wimpy that sounds?"

"I know," said Joe, hailing a cab. "Just cover for me, okay?"

Frank grinned. "What makes you think I'm any happier about explaining this to Hamaguchi? I know this isn't exactly the 'honorable' way to handle the situation, but I say we go back to the apartment and both call in sick!"

Nearly an hour later Frank opened the door to their cramped apartment. He stepped inside slowly, unable to believe what he saw.

Their cups and dishes had been taken out of the cabinet and smashed to bits. Their books and linen had been ripped to shreds. And the apartment's pristine white walls were splattered with bloodred paint that read "*Gaijin,* go home!"

Joe gave a low whistle of astonishment. "*Gaijin*—that means us, doesn't it?"

Frank nodded. "Someone's trying to warn us off the case. That guy at the warehouse must have put out the word about us being there."

Joe peered into the bathroom and saw that the mirror had been shattered. "Well, whoever sent this message is pretty serious," he commented.

"Well, in a way, it's good news," Frank pointed out. "It means we've found out something that we shouldn't have during our little score at the warehouse today, and maybe that info you called up on your computer, too. We're making the counterfeiters very nervous."

Joe stared at Frank as if he'd lost his mind. "How much more nervous do you intend to make them?"

"A lot," Frank said softly. "One way or another we have to force their hand."

"That all sounds great," Joe said, stopping to pick up some of the broken china. "I'm just not sure I want to be here when we do. We'd better call the police."

"Well?" Bess asked as Nancy emerged from a cubicle in the busy Tokyo police station.

Nancy's blue eyes were grim. "I told Mr. Hartwell that Lettie had seen the vases in one of the hotel linen closets," she reported. "And he told me that the police think she's too confused to be a witness."

"Does this mean they're not going to check out the hotel?" Bess wanted to know.

Nancy sighed. "That's exactly what it means."

Bess led the way outside, where the last rays

of the afternoon sun were casting deep shadows on the pavement.

Glancing at her watch, Bess told Nancy, "Um, I hate to say this, but it's almost dinner-time."

"I know, I know," Nancy said, smiling. "And I wouldn't dream of keeping you from your date with Hiro. Anyway, I promised to meet Frank and Joe for dinner. I'll see you back at the room."

Nancy made her way to the noodle shop where she'd agreed to meet the Hardys. Frank and Joe were already there when she arrived, and soon they had steaming bowls of broth, seafood, and noodles in front of them.

Nancy quickly told the brothers about her search for the vases and Hartwell's refusal to take the tip seriously. "It was so frustrating," she finished. "I couldn't just come out and tell him I'd been breaking into linen closets and I'd found proof."

"We're pretty much in the same boat," Frank said after they'd ordered. "We *think* we've found the place where they're switching Amsa Elite components for the inferior ones, but the minute we tell the police how we got into the warehouse, we'll be in major trouble. We can't really tell anyone until we know for positive *who* is behind it."

Joe launched into the story of the warehouse

and their ransacked apartment. "We called Mr. Yamada, but he had been called back to the States on an emergency. So we couldn't tell him about the warehouse.

"His secretary said he would be in touch with us soon," Joe added. "Until then we're pretty much on our own. Since we can't discuss the case, we can't tell the police about our apartment."

Nancy shuddered, "Do you guys feel okay about staying in that place?"

"No," Joe said, letting out a long breath of air, "but we don't have much choice."

"Mmm," said Nancy, sipping a spoonful of the rich, delicious broth. "Anything new at Amsa?"

"This morning Mariko and Kamura were going at it again," Joe told her. "He's condescending to everyone, but with her he's unbelievable. I'm surprised she didn't kill him six months ago."

Frank shot Joe a warning look. "You're feeling awfully sympathetic toward a suspect," he observed.

"You'd feel the same way if you worked in that office," Joe replied.

"You said the guy in that abandoned warehouse was the same one who ripped off Mariko's bag," Nancy said thoughtfully. "So that means he must have been after those schematics she took from Kamura, despite what Mariko told you."

"I think so, too," Frank said. "And if he went after the documents that came from Kamura's desk, then Kamura may be linked to the whole mess."

Joe gave a humorless grin. "Finally we're getting somewhere. I still don't see how Mariko figures in this. I mean, I doubt that she's actually in cahoots with Kamura. But she's definitely up to *something.*"

"By the way," Frank said, "where's Bess tonight?"

"On a date with Hiro," Nancy answered.

"Cupid strikes again," Joe said, fluttering his eyelashes madly.

Nancy grinned. "Look who's talking. I hate to break this up, but it's getting late, and I'd better get back to my hotel. Bess and I leave for Kyoto in the morning."

Wednesday morning Joe had his foot up on the locker room bench and was unlacing his sneaker. He was still breathing hard from Amsa's morning company calisthenics class.

He turned as someone swatted him across the shoulders with a towel. "You are going to Mount Fuji?" Tadashi Kamura asked in his heavily accented English.

Joe hesitated a moment, wondering why

Kamura cared whether he went on the company hike up the famous mountain. "Sure," Joe said. "Is this trip—you know, required?"

"All trainees are expected to go," Kamura said.

Joe peeled off his sweatshirt. "Then I'll be there."

Kamura looked at him contemptuously. "Do you think you are capable of climbing the mountain?"

"I don't think I'll have any problems," Joe replied easily.

Kamura's eyes narrowed. "Do not be so sure."

"What?" Joe demanded, but Kamura was already calling to someone else in Japanese.

"What was that all about?" Frank asked, straddling the bench next to Joe.

"I don't know," Joe said slowly. "I think I was just warned off the mountain."

Frank raised one dark eyebrow. "That's the second warning in two days. If Kamura and that thug at the warehouse are connected, then Kamura knows we were there."

"That's what I was thinking," Joe said. "And that if the counterfeiters know we were at the warehouse, they're probably going to try to move the stuff out before we can return."

"Or," Frank said grimly, "they're going to make sure we never get the chance to return."

Joe and Frank finished changing and took off for their jobs.

Back in the trainees area, Joe sat down at his computer and called up the figures he'd been working on the morning before, a comparison of stereo receiver frequencies. Although he'd worked hard on the analysis, the numbers made no sense.

Well, Joe thought, I can sit here all day getting frustrated or I can ask Mr. Okata for help. He saw that the supervisor's door was shut, and there was no question of bothering him. The one other person who might know the answer was Tadashi Kamura.

Swallowing his pride, Joe forced himself to walk back to Kamura's desk. As usual, Kamura was completely absorbed in what was on his screen. He wasn't even aware of Joe's standing there.

Joe decided this was no time for Japanese etiquette. He stared openly at the screen—then blinked. Kamura was scanning the same list of video game cartridge components he himself had accidentally accessed—paired with the cartridge design specifications. All of it was top secret, the sort of information *no* trainee had access to.

Kamura must have sensed Joe's being there, and his head swiveled around all at once. "What do you want?" he demanded.

"I—I got stuck on some calculations," Joe stammered, hoping Kamura didn't know he'd just seen the video cartridge data. "I wanted to ask you if you could tell me what I'm doing wrong."

Kamura cleared his screen and followed Joe back to his desk.

"Sorry I interrupted you," Joe said conversationally. "What were you working on?"

"You wouldn't understand," Kamura replied curtly, sitting down in Joe's chair. His eyes flicked rapidly across Joe's screen, then went to the printout Joe was working from. "Here," he said, pointing to an error in the data. "This is the problem." He showed Joe how to correct it. In seconds Joe's calculations were working exactly as they should.

"Domo," Joe said. "Thank you." Kamura was already back at his own desk.

That was instructive, Joe thought. Not only did Kamura find my mistake, but I may have found his! Joe didn't know what Kamura's normal work entailed, but he did know that none of the trainees in the company were given design specs on a product as hot as the new game cartridges. Kamura was accessing top secret information. The only reason Joe could think of was that Kamura was counterfeiting the game cartridges.

Joe's mind raced to the document Mariko

had taken from Kamura's desk, the one with the wiring diagrams. She said she'd picked it up by mistake when she grabbed her own report. Was she telling the truth, or had she deliberately taken the document?

Mariko tapped him on the shoulder just then and said, "If Okata asks, tell him I took a break." Before he could respond, she swept out of the office.

Where was she going? Joe wondered. She regularly arrived at work later, left earlier, and took more breaks than the rest of the department combined. Each of those acts was considered a serious breach of etiquette in a Japanese company because it meant that the other workers would have to take up the slack.

What does she do on all those breaks, anyway? Joe asked himself. This time he decided to find out. Ignoring the fact that he wasn't supposed to leave either, Joe went out into the hallway. It was empty.

Joe circled the entire tenth floor before he heard whispered voices. Quietly he approached the narrow entry to one of the conference rooms and peered around the corner.

What he saw made all his suspicions about Jim Yamada's niece resurface. Mariko was standing in earnest conversation with Isao Matsuda.

Isao wasn't even supposed to be on this floor, Joe knew. He was supposed to be down in shipping with Frank. Why were the two meeting secretly? Was Mariko tied to Isao and the *yakuza?* If she was, what was she plotting?

Chapter Twelve

"WHEW!" said Bess as the train they'd just gotten off zoomed out of the Kyoto station. "It's still morning and we're already in Kyoto. I can't believe how fast that thing moves! No wonder they call it the bullet train."

"It does sort of make you feel like you're in the twenty-first century," Nancy said. "Until you see a fifteenth-century building, that is. Sometimes I wonder what year it really is."

Following Hiro's directions, the two girls found the bus stop for the line that would take them to the inn. Nancy watched the streets of Kyoto flash by outside the bus windows. Kyoto was as modern as Tokyo but not nearly so big. Like Tokyo, Kyoto, too, was made up of many small districts.

"This must be the business district," Bess said, checking her guidebook. "There's also a geisha district and an entertainment district, and even one that specializes in pottery shops."

"Oh?" said Nancy. "That's where we start looking for the store where Lettie bought her vase."

The bus let them off in Higashiyama, the eastern district, in one of Kyoto's older neighborhoods. The inn was set on the corner of a quiet street, the grounds edged with cherry trees and pine. "It's beautiful!" Bess exclaimed as she took in the low building with its tiled, pagoda-style roof and carved wooden doors.

A woman dressed in a pale green kimono came to the door as Nancy and Bess approached the inn. *"Konnichi-wa,"* the woman said, bowing. "Good day."

Nancy and Bess returned the greeting, then followed the woman down a step and into a small hallway. There they changed from their shoes into slippers provided by the inn. The hostess bowed again, then led Nancy and Bess along a hall with smooth wooden floors.

At the back of the inn the woman stopped in front of a rice paper *shoji* screen. She slid it to the side, revealing a simple room with its floor covered with straw mats. A scroll bearing bold strokes of Japanese calligraphy hung from one wall. The only furniture in the room was a low, rectangular table and a small wooden cabinet.

"Nancy," Bess whispered in alarm, "there aren't any beds in here!"

The woman took off her own thongs and gestured for the girls to remove their slippers. Then she stepped into the room and opened the door of the cabinet. Inside Nancy saw what looked like rolled-up mattresses and quilts. "The maid will set out your beds tonight," the woman promised. She indicated two cotton kimonos hanging from the wall. "These are *yukatas,*" she said. "Please make yourselves comfortable. Tonight dinner will be brought to your room." She gave another bow and left, sliding the *shoji* screen closed behind her.

Bess eagerly began changing out of her clothes and into the cotton robe. "See," she said, closing the left side of the *yukata* over the right. "Hiro told me you have to fasten it this way. The Japanese only fasten kimonos right over left when they dress a corpse."

Nancy felt herself shudder. "Then definitely wrap it the way he said. Are you going to wear it out on the streets?"

"Hiro says it's perfectly okay."

Hiro says. Lately Bess seemed to use those words in every sentence. This romance was developing awfully fast, but Nancy wasn't about to say that to Bess. She'd never seen Bess as happy as she'd been since meeting Hiro.

So with Nancy dressed in a denim skirt and pale yellow sweater, and Bess in a full-length *yukata* and thongs, the two girls set out to find a vase that matched the one Lettie Aldridge had bought.

Starting in Kiyomizu, the district famous for its pottery shops, Nancy and Bess methodically went into every ceramics and gift shop. By midafternoon they'd seen pottery of every size, shape, color, and use—but none had the distinctive blue-and-white glaze.

"Maybe the shop where Lettie bought her vase isn't in Kyoto," Bess said, sounding discouraged.

"I've been thinking the same thing," Nancy admitted, pausing next to a delicately carved *torii,* a gateway to a Shinto shrine. She glanced down the narrow street they were on. Beyond the *torii,* she could see the pagoda-style roofs of the temple itself.

"There's one more ceramics shop at the end of the street," she said. "We might as well try it."

Bess adjusted her *yukata.* "Might as well. Besides," she added with a giggle, "I like walking around in this thing."

Directly ahead of Nancy and Bess, filing into

the ceramics shop at the end of the street, was the Journeys seniors' tour, Kenji in the lead.

Nancy held her breath as she entered the low wooden doorway that led into the ceramics shop. The shop was crowded with seniors, and yet Nancy easily spotted what she'd been searching for. A shelf by the door was covered with vases, teapots, and bowls, all in the familiar blue-and-white pattern!

Kenji was the first to notice Nancy and Bess. He gave the girls a quick bow and smiled. Then the Olsons saw them, and Nancy and Bess spent the next few moments talking to them.

"May I have your attention?" Kenji spoke up. "We are now in one of Kyoto's most respected ceramics studios. The craftsmen here have been making their pottery the same way for seven generations." He grinned at his group. "Even better, they have an American apprentice who will be happy to explain the process and answer your questions."

I'd love to ask if they're hiding stolen pearls in their vases, Nancy thought. That made her think of something else: Wouldn't the extreme heat of firing the vases damage pearls? Then again, she supposed a false bottom with the pearls could be glued to the vases *after* firing.

A tall young man with curly blond hair and a beard introduced himself as Theo Meredith and began to explain how a bowl was made. Nancy followed the lecture, but it didn't provide her with any clue as to how the pearls might be hidden in the pottery.

After Theo led them back into the studio, Nancy whispered to Bess, "Could you distract him with a question?"

Bess winked at her. "I'll keep him busy."

As Bess began a very long and complicated question about glazing, Nancy stepped away from the crowd and back toward the shelves near the studio door. When she was sure that Theo was concentrating on Bess, she took out the piece from Lettie's vase and held it against one of the vases on the shelf. The pattern and glaze were identical.

Nancy quickly put the fragment away as the tour returned to the front of the shop. Several seniors asked the prices of the items on the shelves, and Nancy wasn't surprised when Theo named very reasonable prices.

"I'd like to buy a vase," Nancy spoke up quickly.

"A pleasure," Theo said. "This one is a real beauty." The vase he offered her was not from the shelf by the door. Instead, he handed her one from beneath the counter.

Nancy frowned. She was sure it was deliberate. If she was right, the vases from the shelf by the door were the ones sold to the seniors, the ones containing the pearls. Seniors made safer, more unsuspecting "mules." On the other hand, the vase Theo had just given her was probably made of clay and glaze and nothing more.

Bess took the vase from Nancy, frowning. "This one is nice," she said, "but I'm totally in love with *that* one." She reached out, grabbed a vase from the shelf by the door, and laid the money for it on the counter.

The smile never left Theo's face as he said, "No problem. Here, let me wrap it for you." As he reached for the vase, Bess pulled it away. "That's all right. I'll take it the way it is," she said. Before he could protest, she sailed out the door, vase in hand.

Nancy paid for her vase, the one that had been stored beneath the counter, then she joined Bess outside. "That was brilliant, Bess!" she said, laughing.

Bess put the vases in her oversize purse. "We've got two of them!" she crowed triumphantly.

"And I can't wait to split them open—"

Nancy broke off as the door to the shop opened and Adele Olson stepped out. "What do you two have planned for the rest of the afternoon?" she asked cheerfully.

"Uh—" Bess began.

"Kenji is taking our group to see the paintings in Chishaku-in Temple," Mrs. Olson went on. "Why don't you join us?"

"We'd love to, but—" Nancy began.

"Don't worry," Mrs. Olson broke in. "I'm sure Kenji won't mind."

"You must come with us," Kenji insisted, joining them. "I wrote two papers on those paintings when I was at the university. You wouldn't want to miss my brilliant theories, would you?"

At the moment all Nancy wanted to do was open the vases to see if they contained stolen pearls. But if Kenji was part of the smuggling operation, she couldn't afford to make him suspicious. "Okay," she finally agreed, "we'll go see the paintings."

At six-thirty that evening Frank was sitting at his desk in the shipping department, tallying yet another stack of invoices. Behind him the other trainees were also still at work.

Frank knew none of them would stop before seven—which was part of what made their investigation so hard. He and Joe spent most of their days at Amsa, with investigative work squeezed into hurried lunch and dinner hours.

Frank lifted his eyes from his work as his supervisor, Mr. Hamaguchi, walked through the office. Hamaguchi was an older man—near retirement, Frank guessed. The supervisor wore his usual outfit, an impeccable navy blue suit with a crisp white shirt. Unlike Mr. Okata, who was nearly fluent, Mr. Hamaguchi spoke little English. Most of what he'd even heard from Hamaguchi were the concise orders he issued with Isao translating.

Mr. Hamaguchi stopped at his desk and picked up a stack of the invoices Frank had already tallied. "Finish?"

"Hai," Frank responded.

Hamaguchi nodded. "Good."

Swell, Frank thought. Great communication here. Could this neat and quiet man be tied into the counterfeiting scam? Was Isao acting on Hamaguchi's orders? As he'd done a million times before, Frank went through a mental list of the others in his department. From what he'd observed, only Isao's behavior was at all suspect. Someone in shipping must be tied in to the counterfeiting, he reminded himself, someone who could get the fakes into the Amsa Elite warehouse.

Unless there was a computer network that connected *all* of the computers in the company? Then it would be possible for someone from another department to modify shipping records. Frank had thought of this before but hadn't checked it out yet.

Frank had a little extra time now and turned on his computer. He used every trick he could think of to identify and enter a net. After an hour and a half of trial and error, he realized that if there was such a net, it was protected by code.

"Frank-san?" Frank looked up as Mr. Hamaguchi approached his desk. "It is late. Others are gone. You go also."

Frank acknowledged the order with a quick bow of his head. He shut down the computer and left the office a few minutes later. Before going home, however, he decided to make one more stop: Mr. Yamada's office. Perhaps the vice president had left a phone number for him to call. If he had, Frank could ask about getting into the computer system.

As Frank had expected, Mr. Yamada's personal secretary was still in. "Did Mr. Yamada call with a message for me or my brother?" Frank asked.

"I'm sorry," she replied. "There is nothing."

Nancy pushed aside the last of the tiny china bowls filled with fish, rice, and vegetable delicacies. "I can't eat another bite," she said.

"I could," Bess said promptly. "I feel like we walked over half of Kyoto today."

"Seven different shrines," Nancy agreed, rubbing a sore calf muscle. "I never want to move again." She glanced longingly at the futons that had been unrolled for their beds. "Except to sleep."

Still, there were the vases to inspect. "Let's take a look at—"

Nancy stopped speaking as she realized Bess wasn't listening to her. She was standing at the window that looked out into the garden.

"What is it?" Nancy asked.

Bess pointed, and Nancy saw a man's silhouette outlined clearly in the shadows. He was crouching in the garden, facing their room.

"S-someone's hiding out there," Bess stammered. "And he's watching us!"

Chapter Thirteen

NANCY'S HEART began to hammer as she watched the shadow of the man crouched outside their room.

"What do you think he's doing out there?" Bess's voice trembled.

"I don't know," Nancy answered, "but I'm going to find out."

"Why don't we just call the innkeeper?" Bess suggested.

Nancy shook her head firmly. "No, that'll give whoever's out there time to get away."

Bess gulped hard and tightened the belt on her *yukata.* "Then I'm coming with you."

"You're sure?" Nancy asked gently.

Bess nodded.

"Then we'd better hide the vases."

"Where?" Bess demanded.

There was no good hiding place in the sparsely furnished room, Nancy realized. She just thrust the vases into the cabinet before leading the way out of the room and moving quietly through the hall toward the front door.

Outside, a few stone lanterns lit the path around the inn, their fires flickering in the cool wind that blew through the trees. Nancy waited a moment for her eyes to adjust to the dark before moving around to the back of the inn.

"This is spooky," Bess murmured, jumping as a pine bough brushed her arm. The crescent moon slipped behind the clouds, and the path became even darker. "What's that?" she whispered.

Nancy heard it, too—a faint rustling. There was definitely something or someone out there with them.

"I wish I had a flashlight," Nancy murmured. "I feel like I'm stalking a ghost."

"Don't mention that word." Bess's voice quavered. She stumbled over the hem of her robe and gave a little gasp of alarm. "Nan," she said unsteadily, "I want to go back inside."

"Okay," Nancy said. "I'll be in soon."

Bess shook her blond head stubbornly. "I'm not leaving you out here all alone with—*it.*"

"Just give me a few more minutes," Nancy whispered. She continued to move toward the back of the inn, trying to figure out which room was theirs.

She bit back a shriek as something small and furry darted around her ankles, knocking her off balance. She went down with a thump.

Nancy got to her feet with a sigh of disgust. If someone was out there, he couldn't have helped hearing her fall. She couldn't take anyone by surprise now. "Let's go back in," she said. "I think I could use one of those famous Japanese baths."

As she and Bess neared their room, however, Nancy forgot all about a bath. The polished wood floor was littered with jagged pieces of rice paper. The screens forming the walls of their room had been slashed.

Bess's voice was horrified. "Oh, Nancy. Our beautiful room—"

"Has been ransacked," Nancy finished, "while you and I were chasing shadows. Bess, would you get the innkeeper, please?"

Bess nodded and hurried off. Nancy went straight to the cabinet, a feeling of dread in the pit of her stomach. As she'd expected, the two ceramic vases were gone.

Joe arrived at work early on Thursday morning. His eyes immediately went to his supervisor's office. The door was open, and the office deserted. Good, he thought, Mr. Okata's not in yet. Only two people were there—Mariko and Kamura. From what Joe could tell, they were in the middle of a major argument.

Mariko stood beside Kamura's desk, her eyes flashing. "Where did you get this schematic?" she demanded in a low voice.

Joe watched as Kamura reached for the paper. He never came close to touching the diagram because Mariko deftly pulled it out of his reach. "Where did you get it?" she repeated.

"All that matters," Kamura said calmly, "is that you just took it from my desk. Therefore, it is my property, and you are a thief."

Mariko sat on the edge of his desk. "Fine," she said. "If you won't answer me, I'll ask Mr. Okata where you got this information."

"Do you think he'll listen to *you?*" Kamura jeered. "You're female and an American."

"And you're a sexist—"

"You ought to be working as a secretary," Kamura went on dismissively. "Everyone in the company knows how poor your work is."

"Not me," Joe put in. "I think she's good at what she does."

Mariko didn't look grateful for his intervention. "Joe," she said, "I don't need you to fight my battles."

"I know you do fine on your own," Joe said.

He was faster than Mariko and snatched the

schematic from her hand. It *was* the wiring diagram for the new gaming cartridges. "Tell me, Kamura," Joe said, "how'd you ever get access to this stuff?"

"Give that back to me!" Mariko ordered, her face white with fury.

"Later," Joe promised. His eyes slid to Kamura, who didn't look the least bit alarmed. What was going on here? he wondered. Why were *both* Kamura and Mariko so interested in the schematic—unless they had some kind of warring partnership in the counterfeiting scheme.

"I don't owe either of you an explanation," Kamura said in a level tone. "But when Mr. Okata comes in, I'm going to report you, Mariko, for taking documents from my desk."

"Does that mean you're willing to tell him *which* document?" Mariko challenged.

Kamura held up a spread sheet, a routine analysis. "I'll say it was this one. Okata will believe me. Too bad your uncle's not here to protect you any longer."

In an instant Mariko was off the desk, looking as if she'd deck Kamura.

Joe intervened again, this time putting his hands on her arm. "Come on," he said gently, "it's time you and I had a talk."

Mariko glared at him but let herself be led out

of the room. They didn't speak as Joe steered her through the halls, crowded now with Amsa employees.

"Where are we going?" Mariko asked when Joe pressed the elevator button.

"Somewhere outside this building."

"Okata will mark us late," she objected.

Joe gave her a sideways glance. "Since when has that bothered you?" he asked. With one hand on Mariko's arm and the other holding the schematics, Joe made his way toward a coffee shop.

"You know," he began cautiously when they were seated in a booth with coffee, "I can't figure you. There have been times when I could have sworn we were friends. Now you're glaring at me like I'm the enemy."

"You're interfering" was her cold reply.

"With what?" Joe asked.

Joe wasn't about to back down. Holding out the schematic, he said, "This is the same wiring diagram you took from Kamura's desk, the same one that was ripped off by that guy. How'd you get it back?"

"I didn't," Mariko said grudgingly. "Kamura did. It was on his desk when I came in this morning."

Which seemed to link Kamura to the thug in the warehouse who had stolen Mariko's bag, Joe realized. "So you saw it on his desk and took it a second time. You wanted to know where Kamura got it. Why? What do you care?

"Why are you so interested in this diagram?" Joe persisted. "And why did you get so angry when I took it?"

"Give it back," she said flatly.

"Tell me why, and I'll think about it," Joe countered.

Mariko stared into her coffee, making a prolonged production of emptying a sugar packet into the cup.

"Come on, Mariko," he pressed. "Why?"

She shrugged again. "Maybe I don't like Kamura, and I wanted to make him uncomfortable."

"That's all?" Joe asked softly. "You were just being mean?" He pushed aside his coffee cup. "I guess I don't know you. I didn't think you'd act that low."

With an impatient sigh, Mariko said, "You're right, you don't know me. Just give back the schematic and we can forget this whole boring conversation, okay?"

"No," Joe said. He didn't know what to say next. He was beginning to wonder if he'd ever figure out how Mariko fit in to the counterfeiting scheme.

"What do you want from me?" she demanded.

"The truth," Joe told her. "Why do you go

out of your way to antagonize everyone at Amsa? And why are you so interested in a wiring diagram."

Mariko stared down at the table, her face hidden by her glossy black hair. At last she looked up. "I'd like to tell you," she said quietly. "It would be nice to have a friend over here. But"—she spread her hands in a gesture of helplessness—"there are things I have to do on my own."

She stood up. "I hope you'll give that back to me," she said, nodding at the schematic. "But I won't pay for it with a confession." With that she turned and left the coffee shop.

Nancy watched as Bess paced the inside of the Kyoto branch of an American bank. "Why did they have to steal our traveler's checks, too?" Bess said as she circled Nancy.

Nancy glanced at her watch—it was nearly two in the afternoon. "I can't believe how long it's taking to get the replacements. Maybe the thief took our traveler's checks just to make sure we'd be busy all day."

"I'll bet the thief's name is Theo Meredith," Nancy said a little later. "Unless it was someone he sent. What I can't figure out is how he knew where we were staying. The only one who knew we were at that *ryokan* was Hiro."

"Whom we can trust," Bess said. "Maybe we were followed." She gave a little shudder.

Two hours later, traveler's checks in hand, the girls decided to return to the ceramics shop. Bess squinted at the sign in Japanese that hung on the door of the shop. "Do you think that says Closed?"

Nancy peered into the darkened shop. All the vases had been put away; the shelves were empty. "Good guess."

"Maybe they'll be open later," Bess said optimistically. "Why don't we go visit a shrine or something and come back?"

Nancy checked her watch. It was nearly four o'clock, and she wanted to get back to Tokyo that night so that she could talk with the seniors in the morning. She didn't really expect the ceramics store to reopen so late in the day, but she was willing to give it a chance. "One shrine," she agreed. "Which one?"

Bess opened her guidebook to a picture of rock gardens edged by lily-covered pond. "I can't pronounce the name," she said, "but it's a Buddhist temple. The gardens there are supposed to be amazing."

When they reached the temple, Nancy had to agree with Bess's description. From the moment she and Bess entered the grounds, she felt transported to another world.

The day was cool and overcast. The trees and temple buildings and gardens were all shrouded in a soft, gray mist. The rock gardens were unlike anything Nancy had ever seen. Small, smooth stones had been raked in whirling patterns, surrounding single boulders, as if they were water and the boulders were islands.

Other tourists moved quietly through the gardens. The only sound came from the largest of the temple buildings. Nancy couldn't be sure, but the low, rhythmic droning sounded like chanting.

Bess nodded in the direction of a slim young Japanese woman ahead of them who wore heels, a stylish wool suit, and gloves. "I'm going to ask her a question—in Japanese," Bess said.

"In Japanese?" Nancy repeated.

Bess grinned. "I figure if I'm going to come back to Japan to see Hiro, I might as well start practicing."

"Might as well," Nancy agreed.

Bess approached the woman and tried to ask her a question. The woman replied politely, but from the look on Bess's face, Nancy guessed that she hadn't understood a word.

"That was really strange," Bess said, rejoining Nancy.

"What was?"

"That woman's wearing a scarf," Bess said.

"But when we were talking it opened a bit, and she—she had an Adam's apple!"

Nancy peered at the woman more carefully. Her face was mostly hidden by the hat and scarf she wore. Nancy couldn't see an Adam's apple, but the woman's hands were unusually large. She brushed a strand of hair out of her eyes. There was something odd about the way she moved the small finger on her right hand.

Nancy looked more closely. The shape of the finger was strange, too, puffed out and unnatural looking at the tip. *The glove was stuffed.*

Suddenly Hiro's comment on the Kabuki actors came back to Nancy, and she understood what she was seeing.

"Bess," she whispered, "that's no woman. That's the *yakuza.*"

Chapter Fourteen

BESS'S FACE completely blanched. "He's going to kill us," she whispered to Nancy. Her voice rose a note. "Right in the middle of this gorgeous garden!"

"No one's going to murder anyone," Nancy said firmly. She led Bess a short distance away from the *yakuza,* trying to remain calm. "Let's just walk a bit and see what happens."

They crossed a stone bridge arching over a stream. "Nan, do you think it's possible he's been following us all along?"

Nancy couldn't lie to her friend. "Well, maybe since yesterday. If he was the thief," she went on curiously, "he's got the vases. What would he want with us now?"

"I don't want to know!" Bess wailed.

"I've got to tie my sneaker," Nancy said, kneeling down. She didn't really, but it gave her a chance to look behind her. As she'd guessed, the fine-featured "woman" was following at a distance.

So we're playing cat and mouse, Nancy thought. The only problem is, the game is pretty terrifying. "Bess," she said as she stood up. "I need to know if he's really after us. I want to draw him out."

"What do you mean?" Bess asked nervously.

Nancy headed uphill along a path that overlooked the lily pond. "I'm going to run," she explained. "I want to see if he breaks cover and follows me."

"So he can get you alone and kill you? That's the worst plan I've ever heard!"

"There are tourists all over the place," Nancy pointed out. "I don't think he'll do anything. Besides, I'm wearing sneakers, and he's wearing heels, so I've got an advantage."

Bess grabbed her arm. "Please, Nan," she said, "don't do this."

Nancy nodded toward the main temple building. "Will you go get help? Just in case."

Bess wasn't convinced, but at last she agreed to Nancy's plan and hurried off. Nancy was relieved to see that the *yakuza* wasn't following Bess. Deliberately, Nancy turned back in the direction of the main building. They had come quite a distance from it, she saw uneasily. Worse, although there had been plenty of tourists five minutes ago, the area had suddenly cleared. It was just she and the *yakuza.*

She walked slowly at first, pretending to admire the delicate pavilion that rose from the center of the pond. She turned, as if to get a more sweeping view of the mist-covered water. The *yakuza* was still trailing, also studying the pavilion.

His disguise is uncanny, Nancy thought. If Bess hadn't seen his Adam's apple, we never would have known he was a man. Now it's time more people found out.

Suddenly Nancy broke into a full sprint, running as fast as she could toward the main temple building. She had only to hear the heels behind her to know that the chase was on. She risked a glance back and saw a glimmer of gray metal in his hand. Was it a knife or a gun? It didn't really matter. Either was deadly.

Where is everyone? Nancy wondered frantically. She cut across a flower bed and darted through a stand of pines, the *yakuza* gaining on her.

The main temple building was now in sight. Nancy raced up to the two great wooden doors that led to the temple and pulled on the iron handles. The doors didn't budge. "Please," she cried, pounding on the wood. "Open up!"

She listened for a response and was greeted with silence. Where was Bess?

Nancy turned. The elegantly dressed "woman" was walking calmly along the path toward Nancy, the metal still glinting in his hand. There was no one else in sight.

Nancy knew she had only one choice. In front of the temple was a large bronze bell. The temple brochure had said that it was rung only for special ceremonies by the Buddhist priests. It specifically warned visitors not to touch it. Running over to the bell, Nancy hefted the heavy bronze hammer from its supports and struck the bell as hard as she could.

A deep, almost eerie, tone resonated through the air. Nancy could feel the vibrations move through her body. It was as if the sound had some sort of power.

Immediately the *yakuza* vanished into the trees. A moment later the doors to the temple swung open, revealing an elderly monk, Bess at his side.

"Thank goodness you're all right!" Bess cried, running over to Nancy.

The monk studied Nancy with a stern gaze. "Come, child," he said in heavily accented English. "We will help you."

Half an hour later Nancy and Bess sat sipping green tea in the nearly bare room that served as office for the *roshi,* the head of the monastery.

He was the same monk Bess had summoned. The *roshi* had listened to their story, then sent a group of monks to search the grounds for the *yakuza*. There was no one found.

"I didn't expect there to be," Nancy said with a sigh.

"Thank you for helping us," Nancy told the elderly monk. "I'm sorry if we caused a disturbance."

"It was nothing," the *roshi* replied. "You are returning to Tokyo by train tonight?"

"Yes," Nancy told him.

"Then I will have several monks escort you to the station."

"Thank you," Nancy said at once, "but that's not necessary. Bess and I—"

"You are in danger here," he told her. "You will please give me the peace of mind of knowing you boarded the train safely."

Beside her, Nancy saw Bess smile and bow her head. "*Domo.* We'd be glad to."

Nancy and Bess returned to their Tokyo hotel just as their Journeys group was returning from a late dinner.

Hiro was the first to greet them. "You're back late," he said, his eyes lingering on Bess. "We missed you. Did you like Kyoto?"

"It was—all right," Bess answered. She and

Nancy had agreed not to mention the theft or chase to anyone in their group.

"Only all right?" Hiro asked, frowning. "What did you see?"

"Actually," Nancy said, "we met up with Kenji's group and tagged along with them."

"Tokyo's been grim without you," Gary whispered, coming up beside Nancy. "Why didn't you take me along?"

Nancy blinked in astonishment. "Take you along?" Nancy saw Wendy watching Gary, her entire body rigid with anger. "I don't think Wendy would have liked it if you went to Kyoto," Nancy said.

"Probably not," Gary admitted. "But I don't need Wendy's permission." One dark eyebrow lifted. "Do you need Ned's?"

"Of course not."

"Then go out with me tomorrow night."

Nancy looked into Gary's light tawny eyes and found herself wanting to say yes. But she couldn't—her first priority had to be solving the case. "Let me think about it," she said finally.

Nancy checked in with the Kyoto police and was told there were no new developments in finding the vases.

"The case might be solved if only we still had those vases . . ." Nancy's voice trailed off.

"Unless one of the seniors in Kenji's group also bought some?"

"Think they'll let you crack one open?"

"I don't know," Nancy said. "I'll leave a message at the desk for the Olsons and see if we can have breakfast together."

The next morning Nancy found that the Olsons had left her a return message, explaining that the seniors were departing earlier than usual for a special trip to the hot springs in Nikko. In fact, when she and Bess reached the lobby, their own group was already assembled and Hiro was giving them instructions for their trip to the Kamakura temple district.

"Remember," Hiro was saying, "if you become separated from the group, take the Yokosuka Line from Tokyo to the Kita-Kamakura stop."

"Right," Wendy said sarcastically. "As if we could remember that. Don't you know all these names sound alike to us?"

Hiro smiled at her. "Then I guess you'll just have to stick with the group."

"How can he be so nice?" Bess whispered to Nancy. "No matter how rude Wendy gets, Hiro acts as if he doesn't even notice her bad manners."

Just then Gary took Wendy's arm and steered her away from the group. From the expression on his face, it seemed he was trying to talk some sense into her.

Nancy and Gary sat together on the train, and across from them, Bess and Hiro were sitting together. Bess was glowing. Nancy watched as Hiro lightly took her hand and said something that made her laugh. For the first time Nancy noticed that both of Hiro's hands bore thick scars across the knuckles.

That's odd, Nancy thought. What could he have done to get such strange scars?

It was late afternoon when Joe, Frank, Mariko, and about thirty-five other Amsa trainees got off the bus that took them from Tokyo to Lake Kawaguchi.

Joe picked up his duffel bag and surveyed the spectacular scenery, his eyes rising to the snow-covered peak of Mount Fuji, towering above the lake. That night they'd stay at a lodge, and the next day they'd rise before dawn to begin their ascent of the mountain.

"It looks just like all the postcards of it," Frank said, staring at the snow-topped volcano.

"Even more beautiful," said Mariko beside him. "They say you can see it from Tokyo on a very clear day, but those days are pretty rare."

"Definitely impressive," Joe agreed. "Almost as impressive as the fact that it's got to be eighty-five degrees here. I say we all go for a swim in the lake."

Mariko was doubtful. "It's still spring. The water will be freezing," she protested.

"You're going to let that stop you?" Joe teased.

"We've got free time till dinner," Frank said. "Let's do it."

Twenty minutes later, after checking into the lodge and unpacking, Frank, Joe, Mariko, and a few of the other trainees met at the lake in their swimsuits.

Mariko cautiously stuck one toe in the water. "It's frigid," she reported, shivering. "There are probably chunks of ice in there. Look."

Joe shrugged, splashed forward, and dove in.

"He's crazy," Mariko muttered.

Frank grinned at her. "Now you're catching on."

Mariko gave a little gasp as Joe, swimming underwater, caught her by the ankles and pulled her off balance. She came up, sputtering water. "You—" she began, using the heel of one hand to send a jet of water at him.

Laughing, Joe held up his hands. "Truce," he declared. "Come on, I'll race you to that buoy out there. You can even have a head start."

"You're on, but you can keep your dumb head start," Mariko told him.

Frank blew an imaginary whistle, and the two

were off. Mariko had no trouble keeping pace with Joe. She was the first to the buoy and the first one back. She stood in the shallows, laughing as Joe swam the last few strokes in to shore.

Joe stood up, shaking the water from his blond hair. "What were you—the star of your high school swim team?" he asked Mariko.

"State swim team," she told him. "And I was captain."

"Figures," Joe said, grimacing. "Well, before I humiliate myself in another race, why don't we do something else?"

"Like what?" Isao Matsuda wanted to know.

Joe looked around. In addition to Frank, Mariko, and Isao, Kamura and three female trainees were also in the water. Just enough, he decided. "Listen up, boys and girls," he said, "your next activity will be chicken fights."

There was a rapid flurry of Japanese as the trainees who didn't speak English tried to decode this.

"Let's show them," Joe said to Frank and Mariko. He boosted Mariko onto his shoulders, and Frank did the same for a girl in the shipping department. With Isao standing below, translating Frank's instructions to the girl on his shoulders, the chicken fight began.

Above Joe, Mariko rocked with peals of laughter. "This is too much," she gasped, "a chicken fight with Japanese subtitles."

"Just push her off Frank's shoulders," Joe muttered. He soon realized it was not going to be that simple. Within minutes everyone in the water had formed chicken-fighting couples, and he found himself doing battle on all sides.

Joe and Mariko were one of the first teams to go down. Joe fell backward, completely submerged, and then decided to swim along the bottom for a bit. It felt good to be in the quiet underwater world after the chaos above.

He surfaced a short time later. Isao and his partner and one other couple were the only ones still standing, Joe saw. Everyone else was gathered on the shore, laughing and cheering them on.

Guess my idea was a success, he congratulated himself. Then he saw Frank's face.

"What's wrong?" Joe asked at once.

"Where's Mariko?" Frank countered. "She never surfaced."

Chapter Fifteen

JOE FELT a cold sensation in the pit of his stomach that had nothing to do with the icy lake.

"Something's happened to Mariko!" he shouted. "Help us look for her!"

The chicken fight stopped immediately, and the other trainees started to search for the girl.

Joe began to dive. Although the lake water was clean, the bottom was muddy. He dove and surfaced more times than he could count, each time finding himself short of breath. Finally, his lungs aching, he made his way back to shore.

"Relax—Kamura brought Mariko in. She's on shore now," Frank said.

"Is she all right?" Joe asked anxiously.

Frank nodded. "She'll be okay."

They cut through the circle of trainees to find Mariko kneeling on the sand. She was shaking and gasping for breath, but she was definitely alive.

Joe grabbed a towel and draped it around her trembling shoulders. "Easy," he said, "you're going to be all right."

Mr. Okata came racing up to them then. He very gently helped Mariko to her feet. "We will send for a doctor," he told her. "Can you walk back to the guest house?"

Mariko nodded. Leaning on Mr. Okata, she began to make her way slowly back to the lodge.

"I don't get it," Frank said as he and Joe watched the others leave the lake. "Mariko used to be captain of her state swim team, so how did she almost drown in a calm lake?"

Joe shivered once. The sun was starting to go down, and there was a chill in the air. "She could have hit her head on a rock when we went down in the chicken fight. Who found her?"

"Kamura."

Joe's jaw tensed. "Did you see him go in after her?" he asked.

Frank shook his head. "We just saw him swimming in with her under one arm."

"Maybe he didn't 'find' her," Joe said. "What if he was with her when she went under?"

"You mean, what if he was the *reason* she went under?" Frank asked.

Joe nodded.

"Kamura gave her CPR," Frank pointed out. "Kind of odd behavior for a killer."

Joe started toward the lodge. "Maybe he didn't want to kill her. Maybe he was just trying to scare her.

"Maybe Mariko knows something about him that Kamura doesn't want anyone to know. This could be his way of warning her to keep quiet." Joe frowned. One way or another, they had to get to the bottom of this—and fast.

Nancy stood next to Gary at the Kita-Kamakura train station. The rest of the Journeys group was somewhere nearby, but she couldn't see them. It was the tail end of rush hour, and the platform was mobbed.

They'd spent the day walking through Kamakura's temple district. Now Nancy was looking forward to getting back to Tokyo, where she and Gary were going to have dinner together.

"At last!" Gary said as the train pulled into the station. He held his hand out to Nancy.

Nancy reached for it. Before she grabbed it, though, someone pushed forward—hard. The next thing Nancy knew, she was stumbling into the train car—alone. A second later the doors slid closed with a *whoosh,* and the train was off.

Nancy stirred uncomfortably, her nose

wedged firmly against the back of a tall man. He moved a bit and she peered around. She couldn't see anyone else from her group. Gary wasn't in sight, nor was Bess, Hiro, or anyone else from the tour. She'd been separated from her group.

She'd heard that Tokyo rush hour trains were so crowded that train attendants actually shoved passengers in until every square inch of the car was filled. Still, she was relatively sure no one else had been pushed at the Kita-Kamakura station—she was the only one who'd flown forward.

Someone had deliberately separated her from her friends. And whoever it was might well be in this car with her.

She gazed around the car again, her heart pounding.

I'm probably being paranoid, she told herself. Being pushed into the train was an accident. No one is going to attack me.

She managed to calm herself down—until she realized she had no idea which Tokyo stop was hers. Hiro had been very specific about the Kamakura stop, but hadn't said anything about the Tokyo station. Nancy closed her eyes, trying to remember the name of her station. It was hard to keep all the Japanese names straight.

The station they'd been at that morning had had red tile on the walls—or was that the one they'd used when they came in from Kyoto the night before? Or did all Tokyo train stations have red tiles on the wall? Nancy felt her heart begin to pound again.

Joe stood outside the hotel, gazing into the night sky. Ahead of him the snow-capped mountain shone under the moon. Joe knew he should be inside resting up for the climb, but he couldn't sleep.

Much as he was glad for the break from office work, it frustrated him that he and Frank hadn't been able to get back to the abandoned warehouse. They should have tried to contact Yamada at least.

He jumped when he heard a soft voice beside him call his name. "Mariko?" he asked in disbelief. He hadn't seen her since Mr. Okata had helped her from the lake.

Mariko slipped out of the shadows to stand beside him. She looked very young and frail in the moonlight.

"Are you all right?" Joe asked.

She nodded. "The doctor said I just had a lot of water in my lungs. They fed me hot soup, and I took a nap. I'm okay now."

"Well, you nearly scared me to death. What happened anyway?"

"I really don't know," she said slowly. "One minute I was up on your shoulders. The next someone pushed us and we went down. When I tried to come up, I couldn't. It was like something was holding me down."

"Or *someone,"* Joe suggested.

Mariko was silent, gazing at the mountain as if she hadn't heard him.

"Mariko," Joe said, "I don't think what happened today was an accident."

The girl turned to face him, her face serene. "Probably not."

"Is that all you're going to say?" Joe demanded. "Someone tried to kill you today!" He wanted to tell her he suspected Kamura, but Mariko probably had come to the same conclusion. Besides, she was still a suspect and to her he was just another trainee.

He ran his hand through his hair in exasperation. He really wasn't in the mood for another conversation in which Mariko politely told him to take a hike. "All right," he said. "I'm glad you're okay. Maybe I'd better turn in now."

"Wait," Mariko called as he headed toward the guest lodge. "I-I'll tell you some of the things you want to know," she offered.

Joe stopped and turned back to her, his expression skeptical.

"My father was Jim Yamada's younger brother," she began abruptly. "His only brother. He was a professor of mathematics, and he and my mother moved to the United States a few years before I was born. My dad taught at Stanford University. Since my uncle was stationed in San Francisco, we saw a lot of him. He was always very protective of our family.

"Then, almost six years ago, my father died of a heart attack. I was thirteen." Mariko hesitated before adding, "And furious. I'd always been a little wild. At least that's the way my mother, who's a very traditional Japanese woman, saw it. And after my father died—well, she thought I was out of control."

"Were you?" Joe asked.

"Not compared to some kids. I didn't do anything dangerous. I dressed the way I wanted and talked back. My grades went from A's to C's in about two months. School just didn't seem to matter."

"So after high school your mother convinced your uncle to bring you to Tokyo for a year as an Amsa trainee?" Joe guessed.

Mariko nodded. "Exactly," she said, smiling. "It was supposed to make a proper, respectful Japanese woman out of me."

"It's working wonders," Joe teased. "So what's the deal with Kamura and the schematics?" he asked, trying to turn the conversation.

"I can't tell you most of it," Mariko said. "If I'm wrong, I'd be disgracing him. Just believe that I'm doing something I hope my uncle will respect me for."

Joe wanted to believe her, but there was still so much that was unexplained—like why Mariko was interested in the schematics in the first place, and what she knew about his computer being erased.

"You've made an enemy of Kamura," he said.

"I'm not afraid of him," she said defiantly.

Joe tried one more time. "Can't you tell me what's going on?"

Mariko shook her head and tilted it up toward his. Joe meant to question her further about Kamura and Isao Matsuda. Instead he found himself lost in her dark eyes. He would never be sure who kissed whom first. Later, all he'd remember was that Mariko tasted like wild mint, and the kiss went on for a long time.

It was well after dinnertime when Nancy finally stumbled into her hotel room. Bess was pacing frantically in front of her bed.

"Where have you been?" cried Bess. "Hiro's out looking for you. I was ready to call the police!"

"I've had a very thorough tour of the Tokyo train system," Nancy replied, easing herself onto her bed. "I got off at five different stations before I found the right one. And that was after being nearly suffocated on the ride into Tokyo."

"Why did you take that train?" Bess asked. "The rest of us waited for a less crowded one."

"I didn't have a choice," Nancy said, frowning as she remembered. "Someone pushed me."

"Are you sure?" Bess asked.

Nancy nodded her head. "I'm just not sure who it was."

"Gary's really worried," Bess went on. "You should call him and let him know you're okay." She handed Nancy a white envelope that was addressed to her. "Here, I think he left you a note. This was slipped under our door."

Nancy unfolded the white piece of paper inside. At the bottom was a red stamp of some sort—Japanese characters enclosed in a circle. But the message was in English.

> You were warned once, Nancy Drew. This is the last warning: Keep to yourself or you'll be very sorry.

Chapter Sixteen

"Do the *yakuza* send poison pen letters?" Nancy wondered out loud.

Bess's brow wrinkled. "I don't know. What's that red thing at the bottom of the note?" she asked, looking over Nancy's shoulder.

Nancy shrugged. "We'll have to get someone to translate."

"And when were you warned before?"

Nancy gave Bess a wry smile. "That depends on what you consider a warning. It could have been that break-in in Kyoto or our run-in with the *yakuza* or the fortune-teller by the Imperial Palace or even getting pushed in the subway."

"Well, I want to know what this *yakuza* connection is all about," Bess said indignantly. "First we see one in the nightclub with the guy

Frank works with. Then the same guy or another one shows up dressed as a woman in Kyoto, following us!"

"What happened in Kyoto was so strange," Nancy mused. "I've been assuming that our room was broken into by someone connected to Theo Meredith and the ceramics shop. Maybe it was the *yakuza;* and maybe the *yakuza* and Theo *are* connected. It makes sense."

"Did Frank and Joe ever figure out what Isao was up to?" Bess asked.

"I don't think so," Nancy replied. "I'd sure love to know how he's connected to my case. *If* he is." She folded the note and put it in her purse. "Tomorrow I'm going to ask someone about the Japanese characters on the note. And since *everyone* seems suspicious to me right now, I'm definitely going to ask someone I don't know!"

Early Saturday morning Frank stared at the top of Mount Fuji and shivered. Although it had been clear the day before, this morning the mountaintop was shrouded in mist. They were right at the base of the mountain now, and what he *could* see wasn't promising: gray-black slag and volcanic rock. He wouldn't call it ugly—it was too impressive for that. But in the dim morning light, Mount Fuji was massive and dark and menacing.

"How far is it to the top?" Frank asked Kamura, who stood near him, pulling on a bright red windbreaker.

"Three thousand, seven hundred and seventy-six meters—over twelve thousand feet. Normally, you can't go up until July. We are lucky that Amsa secured a special permit for our group and we don't have to ascend with the crowds."

"We're going to be the only ones on the mountain?" Frank asked. He didn't know why, but the idea made him uneasy.

Kamura pulled on gloves and a wool cap. "Fuji is Japan's holy mountain, sacred to both the Buddhist and Shinto religions. The Shintos believe it's the seat of the gods, and the Buddhists believe it's the gateway to another world. Except during the dead of winter, there are always a few monks or others climbing it."

Frank felt slightly better as Isao translated Mr. Okata's instructions. Altogether there were thirty-eight Amsa trainees making the climb. According to Mr. Okata, the six- to eight-hour ascent would be an exercise in togetherness, cooperation, and company spirit.

They were about halfway up the mountain when Frank realized it had been a while since he'd talked to anyone. Joe, Isao, Mariko, and Kamura—the only four trainees who were fluent in English—had gone on ahead. A short while later he saw Mariko on the path ahead of him. He was going to call to her, when Isao emerged from the station stop ahead and pulled the girl aside.

Walking as quietly as he could, Frank approached them. Their voices drifted out to him. He only caught two words of their conversation, but they were enough to make him suspicious: *the pearls.*

Mariko's involved with the pearls, Frank thought uneasily, and Joe is involved with Mariko. Lately he'd avoided talking to his brother about Mariko, mostly because Joe was so touchy about the subject. This time, he thought, I can't let it go.

He waited until they reached the next station stop. From the looks of it, Joe had been there awhile. He was sitting on a boulder, finishing a hot drink. "Hey there," he greeted Frank cheerfully. "Having fun?"

"I'm—concerned," Frank replied.

"About what?" Joe asked.

"Mariko," Frank said, taking a deep breath.

Joe's blue eyes narrowed. "Whatever you're going to say—don't. She leveled with me last night—sort of—and I'm starting to trust her."

"You are, are you? If she's so trustworthy, then why did she and Isao just have another little meeting—where they were talking about *pearls!*"

"I don't know why," Joe told him angrily. "And right now I don't care. I think you're just automatically suspicious of any girl I like."

Frank tried to keep his voice level. "You know that's not true. But there happen to be a lot of unanswered questions about Mariko."

Joe finished his drink and stood up, his eyes blazing. "She's starting to trust me, and I'm starting to get answers. I don't need you to ruin things by your insisting that she's a criminal."

"Maybe I don't want to see you get hurt," Frank said, trying another approach.

"Lay off, Frank," Joe warned. "This one is none of your business." Without another word he continued up the mountain.

Frank let him go. There really wasn't anything he could do to stop him. Glancing around, Frank saw that Isao was sitting apart from the others. He was hungrily consuming a stack of rice cakes. Maybe the time had come to ask Isao a few questions.

Frank bought a drink and sat down beside the tall, thin boy. Isao turned to him and asked, "Do you like our mountain?" He was more relaxed than Frank had ever seen him.

Frank stared out over the lakes and green countryside below. "It's a great view," he said, rubbing his hands together. "A little chilly to be climbing, but worth it."

"It will be much colder at the top," Isao predicted.

"Are you and Mariko friends?" Frank asked conversationally."

"She's very beautiful," Isao said wistfully.

So Joe wasn't the only one who had a crush on the headstrong girl, Frank realized. "It's hard to know how to impress someone like Mariko," he said tentatively, feeling out the situation.

Isao laughed. "Tell me about it!"

"You could give her flowers," Frank suggested.

Isao rolled his eyes.

"Or jewelry," Frank went on. "Maybe some earrings. I'll bet she likes pearls."

It was the wrong thing to say. Frank could see Isao shut down. The boy's body tensed, and he dropped his gaze. "I've got to go," Isao mumbled.

Frank decided the only course left was to try to shock Isao into leveling with him. "Don't you want to give her pearls?" he asked. "Or maybe that's unnecessary. Maybe she's in it with you. Maybe you both steal them."

Isao backed away from Frank, his eyes wild with fear. "What are you accusing me of?"

"You didn't steal pearls?" Frank pressed. "Then what did you hand over to that wrestler at the sumo stable?"

"What are you?" Isao demanded. "An undercover cop?"

"I'm a friend," Frank hedged. "I know you're scared. I can help you if you'll let me."

Isao backed away from him, moving unsteadily toward the path. "Stay away," he said. "You stay away from me and from Mariko."

That's when they heard Mariko's screams from above them. "Joe!" she screamed.

Frank ran back to the trail, but he couldn't see any sign of his brother or Mariko. She had called from somewhere above him, so he started up.

"Joe!" Mariko screamed again. A chill ran through Frank at her next words. "Someone help Joe! He's falling off the mountain!"

Chapter Seventeen

FRANK RACED UP the steep mountain trail, pushing past Kamura and half a dozen other trainees.

He stopped suddenly, unable to believe what he was seeing. His arms shielding his head, Joe was rolling down the side of Mount Fuji! There was no way Frank could reach him in time.

There weren't any trees or shrubs to break his fall. But there was a small boulder, almost in his path. Maybe it would do the trick.

Frank's heart nearly stopped as his brother did roll into the boulder. Miraculously, it stopped his fall.

Frank left the path, scrambling down the rocky mountain. He was the first to reach his brother's side. Joe was cut and bruised, but he was alert.

"Don't try to talk or move," Frank cautioned. He tugged off his denim jacket and placed it over his brother. "You're going to be all right. Someone's getting help."

Frank watched as the medics examined his brother and lifted him carefully onto the stretcher. "How is he?" he asked anxiously. "Is anything broken?"

"Necessary to make X-rays," one of the medics replied in stilted English.

As the medics carried Joe down the mountain, Frank sought out Mr. Okata. "I have to go with him," he said, half expecting an argument.

"Of course," Mr. Okata said. "You should have someone with you who speaks Japanese, also. The hospital could be confusing otherwise." He turned and signaled to Tadashi Kamura, who stepped forward.

"Kamura-san," he said, then went on in rapid Japanese.

"I will escort you and Joe to the hospital and help you make necessary arrangements," Kamura said, bowing to Frank.

At the moment Frank had no patience with Japanese formalities. "Please!" he said, gesturing toward the retreating stretcher.

"Go at once," Mr. Okata said. "I'll check in with the hospital later today."

Nearly three and a half hours later Frank, Joe, and Kamura reached the bottom of the mountain, where an ambulance was waiting. Frank and Kamura hadn't talked much on the way down. Any other time Frank would have been glad for the chance to pump him for information, but now he could think only about Joe.

The ride to the hospital was mercifully brief, but the wait in the emergency room dragged on for over an hour.

"Do you want me to ask about him?" Kamura asked finally.

"Please," Frank said. He was almost beginning to like Kamura in spite of all Joe had told him.

Kamura went to the nurses' station and returned a few minutes later. "He's being seen by doctors now. We should hear something soon."

Another hour passed before a white-coated doctor asked for Frank Hardy. Kamura translated the doctor's report. "Your brother is very lucky. He has no broken bones or internal injuries. He is badly bruised and will be sore for a while, but that seems to be the worst of it. However, they would like to keep him overnight to make sure he hasn't suffered a concussion. If there are no further problems, you may take him home in the morning."

"Ask if I can see him," Frank told Kamura.

Kamura relayed the question. "They've given

him something to help him sleep," he said a moment later, "but you may go to his room and sit with him if you like."

Frank nodded and thanked the doctor and Kamura.

"Excuse me," Kamura said. "I must make a phone call." He returned a few minutes later, smiling. "I have just called Amsa; they will send a company car in the morning to bring you and your brother back to Tokyo."

"Domo arigato," Frank said sincerely. "I appreciate all your help."

Kamura gave him a brief bow and said, "I will return to the lodge now—unless you wish me to stay."

Frank said no and thanked him again.

Joe woke up to a doctor prying open his left eye and shining a flashlight into it. When the doctor had finished checking his eyes, Joe saw Frank slumped in a chair beside the bed, sound asleep.

"Frank." Joe groaned as he tried to move his arm to nudge his brother. Everything hurt.

"You should be careful," the doctor said, giving him a stern look. "You need rest, not movement."

"Got it," Joe agreed. He managed to lie very still until the doctor finished, but he was itching to be up and around.

Frank blinked awake a few minutes after the doctor left. "How are you feeling?" he asked.

"As if every bone in my body is broken. Otherwise I feel just dandy," Joe replied with a grin. "The doctor says I can go home once you sign some forms."

Frank yawned and stretched and eyed his brother curiously. "How did you manage to fall off Mount Fuji anyway?"

Joe grimaced. "I didn't fall. I was pushed, and I'd lay money that Kamura was the one who pushed me. I mean, he even warned me I'd have trouble on the mountain."

"Sorry to disappoint you," Frank said, "but it couldn't have been Kamura. He was still down at the rest stop when you went over the edge. I know because I ran right past him."

"You're sure?" Joe asked doubtfully.

"Positive. No one else was wearing a bright red windbreaker. Who *was* near you?" Frank asked. "Can you remember?"

Joe shut his eyes and leaned back against the pillow. "There was only one person," he said. "Mariko."

Nancy towel-dried her hair, still feeling the pleasant warmth of Nikko's hot springs. After the last few hectic days, the outdoor hot springs —complete with tropical ferns and steaming waterfalls—had been a perfectly luxurious way to spend a Sunday morning.

"Do you believe it?" Bess asked, coming to stand beside Nancy in the spa's dressing room. "Michael Ryder actually checked his video camera and went splashing around like the rest of us!"

An attendant entered the dressing room with an armful of clean towels. "Do you need anything?" she asked in heavily accented English.

"We're fine, thanks," Bess answered.

"Excuse me," Nancy said, "could I ask you for a favor?"

The woman nodded, waiting, and Nancy took out the warning note she'd received the night before. Folding it so that only the red-inked Japanese characters showed, she held it out to the woman. "Could you tell me what this means?"

The woman studied it for a moment and frowned. "That is a seal—a kind of stamp we use for our legal signatures. This one shows the characters for *komadori.* In English it means 'horse bird.' "

"Horse bird?" Bess echoed. "What is that?"

The woman shook her head, equally puzzled. "It must be a name."

"Where would someone get a seal like this?" Nancy asked.

"There are many stores in Tokyo where they

can be ordered," the attendant replied, picking up her stack of towels again.

Nancy thanked the woman. She sat staring at the note long after the attendant had gone. Who was Horse Bird? And why was he threatening her?

With Frank at his side Joe slowly made his way toward the black car waiting in front of the hospital. "All right!" he said. "Our own private limo!"

"It's not exactly a limo," Frank pointed out. "More like a sedan with a driver."

"Details, details," Joe said. "I could get used to this kind of life."

"Yeah," Frank said. "All you have to do is fall off a few more mountains, and you'll have it made."

Joe gingerly lowered himself into the backseat of the car. The driver was a burly man who didn't seem to speak any English beyond the word *Hardys.*

As the car traveled back toward the city, Joe's thoughts were on Mariko. Had she really been the one to push him? He couldn't believe it. Not after the way she'd acted the night before.

They'd been traveling almost an hour when the driver suddenly pulled the car off the road and parked at the side of a low cement building. Turning to the Hardys, he spoke another English word—*bathroom.* Then he got out of the car and went into the building.

"Want to go in?" Frank asked Joe.

"No, thanks," Joe replied. "I'm only moving when I have to."

Frank leaned back against the car seat, his arms folded across his chest. A moment later, Joe saw his brother's eyes fly open as he leaned forward intently.

"What?" Joe asked.

"Don't you hear it?"

"What?"

"Never mind what. You have to move!" Frank shouted.

Joe's whole body protested as Frank threw open the car door and dragged him from the sedan. Frank didn't let go of him until they were a long way from the car.

Joe wrenched a very sore arm out of his brother's grip. "Would you mind explaining—" he began.

As he spoke there was a loud *whoosh* and then a deafening explosion that sent both boys flying backward.

Joe hit the ground hard and waited for the pain to subside a little before he raised his head. Hot yellow flames were shooting from the car's windows.

"I don't believe it," Joe murmured. "Our car just blew up!"

Chapter Eighteen

FRANK COVERED HIS HEAD as a deafening crack filled the air and chunks of burning metal flew from the exploding car.

"We've got to get out of here!" he cried. "Are you hurt?" he asked his brother.

Joe shook his head. "No worse than I already was," he said with a weak smile.

"Then let's go." Frank helped Joe to his feet and pulled him toward the road. "I'd love to find that driver, but we've got to get another ride and fast!"

Joe turned for one last look at the burning car. "That's why the guy parked so far from the building."

Frank put a thumb out. "I wonder if hitchhikers use a thumb in Japan," he mused.

"We were set up," Joe said. "Kamura called for the car. He arranged this. He's got to be the one behind the counterfeiting. He knows we're onto him, and he ordered this."

"How about Mr. Okata?" Frank asked. "After all, he's the one who assigned Kamura to go to the hospital with us."

"You know this means we can't go back to Amsa," Joe said slowly. "They've shown their hand, so now they'll have to finish us off."

Frank nodded. "I say we go to the only people in Tokyo we can trust," he said. "Nancy and Bess."

At last a red convertible stopped. The driver was a Japanese guy who looked to be about Frank's age. He was wearing jeans and sunglasses, and American rock 'n' roll blasted from the car's speakers. "Americans?" the boy asked eagerly.

"As apple pie," Frank told him. "We're trying to get to Tokyo."

"Radical!" the boy declared, his smile becoming even wider. "You get in. I practice my slang."

"What are you going to bring back for your dad?" Bess asked Nancy as they made their way through the crowded streets of the Ginza shopping district on Sunday afternoon.

"I'm not sure," Nancy said. "I was thinking of a lacquered pen set."

"Bor-ring!" Wendy declared from behind the two girls.

Nancy ignored the comment, as she'd ignored countless others that day. She, Bess, Hiro, and Gary had decided to take one of the tour's free afternoons to shop for gifts. Wendy had insisted on tagging along, and she'd spent the entire afternoon directing cutting remarks at Nancy.

"I think a pen set sounds great," Bess said.

Hiro led them to one of Ginza's tiny specialty shops, and Nancy bought a beautiful brown lacquered pen and ink set for her father, as well as handmade stationery for their housekeeper, Hannah Gruen.

"What's next?" Hiro asked.

"I'm still trying to find the right kimono," Bess said. "All the ones I like are too expensive."

Once again Hiro led them to a tiny shop tucked away on a back street. "The kimonos here are secondhand," he explained. "But they're of excellent quality."

Bess and Wendy immediately began to sort through the racks of silk garments. "These are gorgeous!" Bess exclaimed. She held a pale coral kimono against herself and sighed contentedly. "I think it's me!"

"Definitely," said Nancy. "The color's perfect." The sound of fabric ripping several feet behind her startled her.

Immediately the man who owned the store stepped out from behind the counter, waving his hands and speaking angrily in Japanese.

Hiro intervened and asked the group what had happened.

Wendy held up a short red kimono with a ragged gash down the front. "Nancy ripped it," she replied.

Nancy whirled on Wendy. "What did you just say?" she asked, outraged.

"Wendy Robin Wohl, that's enough!" Gary broke in, his face red with anger. "Pay for the kimono and apologize to Nancy."

"You sound like my father," Wendy shouted.

"Now!" Gary told her.

Nancy had had all that she could take. She didn't want Wendy's apologies; she just wanted to get away from her. So she excused herself and set off for the hotel.

Half an hour later she was sitting on the edge of her bed, shaking with fury.

A knock sounded on the door, and Nancy opened it to find Gary standing there. "I'm sorry—" he began.

"Why should you be?" Nancy asked. "You're not responsible for her."

"No, but sometimes I feel I am. Could I come in for a minute?

"Wendy got into trouble at college this winter," he began once he was inside the room. "She got herself kicked out of school and has been living at home ever since. When her parents found out my folks had offered me this trip, they decided to send Wendy along—mostly to get her out of their hair."

"She's in love with you," Nancy said. "That's why she's been so obnoxious to me."

Gary shrugged. "She's going to have to get over that. I've never pretended that we were anything more than friends. I'm really sorry she's been so awful to you. I don't know what else to say."

"It's all right," she told him. "You don't have to say anything else. I just need some time alone, okay?"

Gary nodded and left. Nancy barely had five minutes to herself before there was another knock on the door. Not again, she thought.

Her annoyance turned to surprise as she opened the door and saw Frank Hardy and a very white-faced Joe.

"Nan, can we come in?" Frank asked, his tone urgent. "We need your help."

"Of course," Nancy told him. She and Frank quickly settled Joe on her bed, then she called room service for some food.

"All right," she said, "now tell me what's happened."

"Our cases must be linked," she said after she'd heard them out. "I'm not sure about Kamura, but it sounds as if Isao and maybe Mariko are linked to the pearls. Plus the *yakuza* is mixed up in the pearls, and we know Isao is probably linked to *yakuza.*"

"Yeah, but is there an actual connection between the pearl smuggling and the counterfeiting?" Frank wondered.

"Maybe tomorrow is the day to find out," Nancy said thoughtfully. "Our tour will be going to Kyoto, and I intend to go back to that ceramics shop." She smiled mischievously. "What if you two just happened to meet us there?"

"Good idea," Frank said, "but we have to get back to that warehouse before they move the operation to another site—if they haven't already."

Joe stood up, wincing. "Let's just go to the warehouse now. Then we can go to Kyoto tomorrow with Nancy."

"Are you crazy!" Nancy and Frank said together.

"Joe," Frank said patiently, "you can barely walk. The doctor said you have to rest. You've got to give yourself at least a day to heal before we call on our friend with the *bo* again. Besides, right now I'm calling Mr. Yamada in San Francisco."

Joe winced. "What are you going to tell him about Mariko?"

"That she pushed—"

"No," Joe insisted. "We don't know that for sure. And we don't really understand the pearl connection. Just don't say anything about her for now, okay?"

Frank didn't look persuaded, Nancy noticed.

"If you do say anything," Joe went on, "I swear I'll go to that warehouse myself right now."

"All right, all right," Frank relented. "We'll wait on Mariko. But when we get this mess worked out, we tell Yamada everything."

Nancy and Joe listened as Frank placed a collect call to Mr. Yamada, only to be told that Mr. Yamada wasn't in and would have to call him back. "There's one more thing," Frank said into the receiver, "could you tell him that it's really important that we get a portable computer with a modem ASAP?" He left Nancy's name and hotel phone number, then hung up.

"Why the computer?" Nancy asked.

"We can't go anywhere near Amsa," Frank explained, "but if I have a computer with a modem, I may still be able to plug into their computer system. So now it's a matter of waiting to hear from Yamada."

"I'm restless," Joe said. "Let's go sightseeing."

Nancy and Frank exchanged disbelieving looks.

"You know what I've always wanted to see?" Joe went on eagerly. "A Japanese *dojo.* I'd love to see a real Japanese karate school."

Nancy sighed. "It would be a fairly passive thing to do," she said. "I'm not sure we can just walk into those places, though. Let me call the concierge. Maybe she knows of a school where they'll let visitors observe."

An hour later, following the concierge's directions, the three friends arrived at one of Tokyo's largest karate schools.

"Will you look at all those black belts?" Joe said as they took seats in the visitors' area. A class was about to begin, and the training floor was filled with students who were stretching, sparring, and practicing.

Nancy's eyes lingered on a young man at the edge of the room. Three narrow gold bars edged the tip of his belt. From her own karate training, Nancy knew that meant he was *san dan,* or third-degree black belt. He was working out on a *makiwara,* a wooden striking board.

In Nancy's karate school the *makiwara* had been padded and students wrapped their hands before using it. This board was bare wood and the black belt was punching it barehanded. Nancy watched, mesmerized, as twenty, forty, sixty times he drove his bare knuckles full force into the hard wood.

How can his hands take that? she wondered. Any normal person would have wound up with broken bones.

Then she understood. Holding a third-degree black belt meant he'd been training intensively for at least ten, possibly fifteen years. He'd probably been hitting the *makiwara* like this since he was a kid. His knuckles weren't bleeding or injured because they were completely callused and scarred over.

Suddenly Nancy's mind flashed on the tough scars she'd seen on Hiro's hands. Now she realized exactly where he had gotten those scars. He had to be a black belt, and a pretty advanced one.

Nancy thought back over the time they'd spent together. Hiro had told her and Bess a lot about his life, and yet he'd never mentioned the martial arts. Why would he hide something that had to be a very big part of his life?

Maybe he just doesn't talk about it, Nancy told herself. But the nagging thought wouldn't leave—was Hiro hiding something?

The three friends returned to the hotel, where a package was waiting for Frank at the front desk, marked in care of Nancy.

"I'll bet this is my computer," said Frank, taking the big rectangular box.

When they got to the room, Bess was there, wearing her new coral kimono.

"That looks great," Joe told her.

"So does this," Frank said, opening the package. "One state-of-the-art Amsa Elite portable computer complete with software and a modem!"

The phone rang, and Nancy picked it up. "For you, Frank," she said. "It's Mr. Yamada."

While he was on the phone, Nancy and Joe explained to Bess what had happened during and after the Hardys' trip to Mount Fuji.

"Joe, you could have been killed!" Bess gasped when they were done. "I'm glad you made it back here."

Frank finished his conversation and immediately turned on his portable computer.

"What are you doing?" Bess wanted to know.

"Soon as I connect the modem to the phone jack, I'll be hooking into Amsa's computer system long-distance," Frank explained. "Mr. Yamada told me how to get into the company's net."

Joe shut his eyes. "Why didn't he tell us that when we started this investigation?"

"Apparently, the net is only used for high-level security matters. Access is something Yamada couldn't give out unless it was absolutely vital. Besides, getting into the company net is just a start. Most of the data files are protected by individual codes."

Frank looked at his brother. "That explains how your hard drive was erased without anyone touching your computer. It's not easy, but it can be done from another terminal if the computers are linked."

"So what are you trying to find?" Bess asked.

"A way into Kamura's files, and maybe Mr. Okata's as well. I need to find those specs Kamura had on the video game cartridges—the stuff that's supposed to be top secret. Hopefully there'll also be information about the second-rate parts they're putting into the counterfeits."

"Yamada told you how to break through the protective codes?" Joe asked.

"Not exactly," Frank replied. "I'm setting up a loop—it will merge with the Japanese dictionary and keep trying various combinations of characters until it hits one of Kamura's passwords. When it does, it will open his files."

Nancy's blue eyes widened. "I thought there were almost two thousand characters in the Japanese alphabet."

"There are," Frank said, grimacing. "I never promised we'd crack the code *quickly*. This program will probably have to run all night." He looked at Nancy apologetically. "It's not safe for us to go back to our apartment tonight—"

"Don't worry, you guys can stay with us," Nancy assured him.

Just then the phone rang again, and Nancy picked it up.

"That was the main desk," she reported a minute later. "They said there's a package down there for me. I'm going to get it. Does anyone else want something from the lobby?"

"No, thanks," Bess answered. Joe and Frank were both staring so intently at the computer screen that they didn't even answer.

Nancy headed out into the hallway. She pressed the button for the elevator and waited. And waited. It must be stuck somewhere, she realized. It's taking forever.

With a shrug she headed for the stairway and began the long walk down to the lobby. The stairwell was brightly lit, but from the moment she entered it, Nancy had a feeling that she wasn't alone. She glanced behind her but didn't see anyone.

As she continued down, the feeling intensified. This is silly, she told herself. As the exit for the next floor came into view, she decided she'd get out of the stairwell and try the elevator again.

Nancy pulled the heavy door open, but she never made it into the corridor. Strong hands suddenly grabbed her from behind.

Reacting instinctively, she tried to drive her

elbow into her attacker—and found her arms pinned. She took a deep breath, ready to shout, but a powerful hand pressed hard against the side of her neck, making it impossible for her to utter a sound. She couldn't even breathe.

Nancy wanted to fight but couldn't. Her body wouldn't respond. The door in front of her seemed very far away, and the brightly lit stairwell was going dark. She was passing out.

The last thing Nancy remembered was her jaws being forced open and a burning liquid being poured down her throat.

Chapter Nineteen

"WAKE UP, Sleeping Beauty."

Nancy blinked drowsily. The voice was familiar but it seemed so far away. Someone was shaking her gently.

"Come on, Nan. Time to wake up."

Nancy forced her eyes open and saw Frank Hardy sitting above her. Joe and Bess were beside him.

"Why are you all watching me sleep?" Nancy wondered. She closed her eyes again. Her body felt heavy, and she was exhausted. She was only dimly aware of someone knocking on the door, and then of a woman's voice in the room.

"Nancy." This time it was Bess. "Please try to sit up. The hotel doctor wants to look at you."

"It's all right," said the woman's voice. "Let her lie as she is."

Cool hands took Nancy's pulse, then felt along her head and throat. A light was shined in her eyes, and something that felt like a cold metal disk was pressed over her heart. "Can you sit up?" the doctor asked.

"I think so," Nancy mumbled. But it was only with help from Frank and Joe that she eventually sat up against the headrest. She opened her eyes, blinking until she focused.

"I think someone applied pressure to your carotid artery, causing you to lose consciousness," the doctor said. "Whoever it was knew what he was doing—otherwise you would be dead."

"Something was forced down my throat," Nancy said as the memory of the attack returned.

"Yes," the doctor agreed. "I think you've been drugged. I'll have to take a blood sample to be certain." She efficiently drew a vial of blood. "See if you can stand up."

Moving very slowly, Nancy got to her feet, swayed for a moment, then righted herself. She took one step, then another. By the time she crossed the room, she felt slightly better.

The doctor watched her progress with satisfaction. "I think you will be all right," she said, "but you will not be able to do much tomorrow.

You must stay in bed. I'll stop by tomorrow afternoon." She looked at Bess. "Make sure she drinks many liquids."

Still feeling dazed, Nancy said goodbye to the doctor, then lowered herself into the desk chair. "Tell me what happened," she said to her friends.

Frank shrugged. "You went to get your package and never came back. We started to worry after you were gone for about twenty minutes."

"So anyway, Frank went looking for you and finally found you in the stairwell, unconscious," Joe continued for his brother. "Then he carried you back here.

"While my brother was being gallant, I went down to the hotel desk and asked about your package."

"There wasn't any?" Nancy guessed.

Joe nodded. "You got it. And they said no one there ever called to tell you there was."

"Then either the desk clerk was lying or someone else placed the call," Bess said, a shiver in her voice. "Nancy, whoever sent you that note wasn't kidding."

"Horse bird," Nancy muttered. "What am I supposed to do with a clue like horse bird?"

The effects of whatever had been poured down her throat were still strong, and Nancy went to sleep almost at once, leaving Frank glued to the computer screen and Bess and Joe bickering about what movie to watch.

"All right!" Frank's triumphant crow woke Nancy from a sound sleep. She opened one eye, picked her head up off the pillow, and put it down again.

She had a killer headache and knew she couldn't go back to sleep. The curtains had been left open, and dawn was just breaking. Frank was still sitting at the desk, Nancy saw.

Joe's head appeared from a pile of blankets on the floor. Peering first at his brother, then at his digital watch, he mumbled, "It's only six A.M., Frank. Go back to sleep."

In the other bed, Bess mumbled something inaudible and rolled over, her blond hair covering her face.

"The loop worked!" Frank said, ignoring the sleepy response from the rest of the room. "It just came up with the password that gets me into all of Kamura's files!"

"And?" Joe asked sleepily.

"Give me a few minutes to see what he's got." Frank's fingers flew over the keyboard. Finally he sat back with a low laugh. "Pay dirt!" he exclaimed softly.

Joe sat up, rubbing his eyes. "What'd you find?"

"Everything we wanted. All the specs for the

video cartridges, plus the specs for the Amsa Elite CD players that were counterfeited," Frank said triumphantly. "That's just for starters. He's also got specs on non-Amsa parts that can be fit into the Amsa casings, and inventory lists for them. And the address on the inventory happens to be that abandoned warehouse."

"Evidence we can actually take to the police," Joe said. Grinning from ear to ear, he pounded a fist into his other palm. "I knew it was Kamura!"

"Don't get too optimistic there," Frank warned. "It definitely is Kamura, but this operation is too complicated for him to have been working solo. He had to have help."

Joe nodded. "Like that goon we met in the warehouse."

"And others," Frank said. "There's just one more thing I have to do." He typed something into the computer and looked up and smiled. "I just left my calling card for Kamura."

Joe stood up and started to stretch. He stopped abruptly, drawing in his breath.

"Still hurting?" Frank asked.

Joe nodded and shrugged.

"I'll let you know after I stand up," Nancy answered. The truth was, she felt terrible. Her head felt as if it were about to split open, and she still had a leaden sensation in every limb.

Maybe I'll feel better once I've been up for a while, she told herself. She got to her feet, put on her robe, and went to the bathroom to wash up. The short walk wasn't very promising.

When Nancy emerged from the bathroom a few minutes later, all three of her friends were up and watching her. "You don't look so hot," Bess said. "Maybe we ought to skip Kyoto today."

"That's exactly what Horse Bird, or whoever did this to me, wants," Nancy said.

"The doctor did tell you to stay in bed," Frank reminded her.

Nancy shook her head firmly. "I can't, Frank. Not today. Look, I'll go down to the coffee shop and have some breakfast. I'm sure I'll feel much better as soon as I eat something."

"You could send for room service," Joe suggested.

"No," Nancy said stubbornly. "I still want to see if I can catch the seniors and find out if any of them bought one of those vases in Theo Meredith's store in Kyoto."

"Joe and I have to get to the police with this information," Frank said, nodding at the computer. "But we'll come back here as soon as we can."

Nancy shook her head. "I'll be in Kyoto."

"Kyoto, then," Frank promised. "Give me the address of that store. We'll meet you there."

Nancy wrote down the address in a shaky hand and handed it to Frank.

By the time she and Bess dressed and went down to the lobby, the seniors' tour had departed for the day. Nancy groaned and headed for the coffee shop. "I feel awful," Nancy confessed.

With an encouraging smile, Bess helped her into a booth. "Have some breakfast," she said. "Maybe that'll help. Then we'll figure out what to do."

Nancy ordered a muffin, a fruit dish, and coffee. When it arrived, she simply sat staring at the food, trying to find the will to eat. At last she forced herself to start with the fruit. "Bess," she said, "did Hiro ever tell you about his training in karate?"

"Hiro?" Bess laughed.

"I think he's trained pretty seriously. I think that's where he got those calluses on his hands. Are you sure he's never mentioned it?"

"Not to me," Bess said, "but I'm not really into that kind of stuff. It'd be like trying to talk to me about football." Bess lifted her head and smiled at something behind Nancy. "Here he comes now. Let's ask him."

"Good morning," said Hiro, coming up to the table and putting a hand on Bess's shoulder. "How are you today?"

He looked at Bess with so much genuine

warmth that Nancy began to wonder if she was making a big deal out of nothing. After all, she reasoned, lots of people have trained in martial arts.

"Hiro," Bess said, "did you ever train in karate?"

Hiro seemed surprised by the question but answered easily. "Almost every boy in Japan trains in the martial arts at one point or another. It's like playing baseball in your country."

Nancy wondered if she should press him about how long he'd trained, but she decided to ask another question instead. Taking the warning note from her purse, she showed Hiro the red stamp. "Could you translate this for me?"

"Literally, it means the horse bird," Hiro said. "But you Americans have a prettier name for it. Our horse bird is what you would call a robin."

"A robin?" Nancy asked, astonished.

"This is a signature seal," Hiro explained, "for someone who is probably American, a woman whose name is Robin. Lots of tourists have name seals made up as a souvenir of Japan."

Nancy remembered Gary yelling at Wendy the day before. He'd called her Wendy *Robin* Wohl. Nancy's mind began to race. Why would Wendy send a warning with the Japanese seal? Obviously, so Nancy would never suspect her, but suspect her of what? Was Wendy the one responsible for what happened last night? Was she somehow tied into the pearl smuggling? Why had she sent the warning?

"Nancy," Hiro said, "are you all right? Maybe you should take it easy today and just stay in the hotel and rest."

Nancy gave a hollow laugh. "You're about the fourth person to suggest that."

"We're going to be doing a lot of walking today," Hiro said. "It may be hard on you."

Was there some reason Hiro didn't want her along? "I'll be fine," Nancy assured him. "Honest."

An hour later, when the Journeys group boarded the bullet train for Kyoto, Nancy was far from fine. Despite the aspirin she'd taken, her head was pounding, and she was still dizzy and exhausted.

Maybe I should have stayed in the hotel. After all, how much detecting can I do when I can barely stand?

Chapter Twenty

IT TOOK FRANK nearly an hour to persuade the Tokyo police to allow him to connect his computer to one of their phone jacks so that he could show them the evidence of the Amsa Elite counterfeiting.

Now two English-speaking officers and a sergeant peered over his shoulder as he called up the data. Occasionally as he worked they consulted among themselves. Do they understand? Frank wondered. And will they believe me?

"Enough," the sergeant announced after a while. "We would like you to take us to this warehouse."

"Happy to," Frank said. Beside him Joe nodded.

Nearly an hour later Frank, Joe, and the three

Tokyo policemen were still a good five miles from the abandoned warehouse. Frank stared out the car window in dismay. He'd expected the police to put on their sirens and slice through traffic. Instead the police car sat snarled in the usual weekday traffic jam.

"I can't believe this," Joe muttered.

When it was twenty minutes since they last moved, Frank suggested to the sergeant, "Uh, maybe we should get out and walk."

"And do what with our car?" the officer inquired politely.

"Perhaps one officer could stay—" Frank began.

"No," the sergeant said firmly. "We go all together."

Finally the traffic began to inch forward, and at last the police car rounded the corner above the warehouse. This time the warehouse didn't look nearly as deserted as it had when he and Joe were last there. A large truck was parked in front of it, and four men were taking cartons from the warehouse and loading them onto the truck.

Frank did a double take when he saw that Kamura was among the men.

"They're clearing out!" Joe exclaimed. "How did we luck out and get Kamura here?"

Frank grinned. "My calling card," he answered. "I left a message on Kamura's computer using the net. I told him I'd meet him here late this afternoon. Apparently he wanted to avoid the meeting. Pretty rude, don't you think?"

The police siren suddenly sounded, and the officers raced from the car, their guns at the ready. The men started running, but were quickly subdued. Frank was dying to get in on the action, but he knew the police would never allow it. From a short distance, he and Joe watched the action.

This part did seem like something from a movie, Frank thought, but he definitely could have used subtitles. The police officers were now asking the four men a set of rapid-fire questions in Japanese and frowning at the answers. The sergeant gave an order, and the four were handcuffed.

Frank noticed that Kamura protested very loudly. When he noticed Frank and Joe, he shot them an angry glare but didn't address them.

"Please," the sergeant said to the Hardys. "Can you identify any of these men?"

Joe pointed at Kamura first. "That's Tadashi Kamura," he said, "a senior trainee in Amsa's research and development department." Next he pointed to the powerfully built man on the right. "He's the one who ripped off our friend's bag and who came at us with the *bo*. I've never seen the other two."

The sergeant gave an order to one of his officers, who opened a large carton addressed to a New York company and began to unpack Amsa Elite video game cassettes.

"You might want to open one up and take a look at the components," Frank suggested. "If it's really an Amsa Elite product, every part will be stamped with their symbol, the crescent in the circle."

The officer opened the casing and said something excitedly to his sergeant. Frank didn't have to speak Japanese to understand they had found counterfeits.

"We have everything we need here to prosecute these men," the police sergeant told the Hardys. "We are most impressed with your detective work, and most grateful for your help. Would you please accompany us back to the station? There are many people who would like to meet you."

Frank exchanged a look with his brother. "I'm sorry," he said reluctantly, "but we have a friend in Kyoto we promised to meet. Would it be all right if we stopped by the station tomorrow?"

The police sergeant bowed. "Would you like us to give you a ride to the train station?"

"No!" Frank and Joe answered together. Seconds later they set off on foot.

* * *

The first stop on the Journeys East tour of Kyoto was Nijojo Castle. Nancy tried to revive her flagging energy as Hiro led them through the five huge palatial buildings.

"This was yet another stronghold for our friend Ieyasu Tokugawa," Hiro explained, "the man who rebuilt the Imperial Palace in Tokyo."

Gary cocked an eyebrow. "Doesn't look like his style," he said in surprise, surveying the low buildings with their pagoda-style roofs. "No moats or guard towers."

"Don't be fooled," Hiro told him. "This was where Tokugawa raised architectural espionage to a high art. By the time he built Nijojo Castle, his personal armies were so powerful that he had no need for exterior defenses. But he was still afraid of treachery. So every building here has hidden rooms where his samurai kept watch for assassins. And even that wasn't precaution enough, so he had 'nightingale' floors laid in all the corridors."

"What are they?" Margot asked.

"They sing," Hiro answered. "Actually they squeak whenever someone steps on them. That way no one could move through the castle unnoticed."

Nancy walked through the elaborate reception halls, guardrooms, living apartments, and audience chambers in a daze. She only made it through the third building before she had to tell

Hiro that she was going to sit in the gardens for a while.

Nancy sat beside a small pond and reflected on the case. Kamura had betrayed everyone at Amsa. Who knew whom Isao was working for? And much as she didn't want to, she had doubts about Hiro and Kenji. Were they deliberately leading the seniors into Theo's ceramics studio so that they could transport stolen pearls? Had they been behind the attack on Nancy and the theft of the vases from the *ryokan?*

"Enjoying yourself?" asked a sharp voice. Nancy was surprised to see Wendy standing about ten feet away.

"Wendy *Robin* Wohl, you're just the person I wanted to see," Nancy said as the other girl walked toward her. "I wanted to thank you for that lovely note you sent."

Wendy paled.

"And for knocking me out last night," Nancy went on. "How did you manage that?"

"Someone knocked you out last night?" Wendy seemed genuinely surprised. "It wasn't me. I was in a club last night. I sent the note and pushed you in the subway, but—" Wendy's hand flew to her mouth as she realized she'd just confessed to another of Nancy's attacks.

"I was wondering about that," Nancy told her. "Why did you do all that?"

Wendy chewed on her lower lip as she decided how much to say. "I—I just wanted you to leave Gary alone," she finally mumbled.

"Why should I believe you aren't the one who knocked me out?" Nancy demanded.

"Ask Margot. She was with me at the club. She wouldn't lie."

Much as Nancy would have liked to blame Wendy, she had a strong feeling that she was telling the truth. "Wendy," she said, "threatening me isn't going to get you Gary. You may have to"—Nancy hesitated—"you have to grow up."

"What? How dare you—" Wendy began defensively.

"There you are!" Bess cut Wendy off, joining them in the garden. "Feeling any better, Nan?"

"Not much," Nancy admitted.

"Well this should cheer you up. Guess what we're doing next?" she asked brightly. "We're going to visit ceramics shops."

The Journeys group took a bus from Nijojo Castle to Kiyomizu, the pottery district. As they began to walk the streets of Kiyomizu Nancy recognized the area from her previous trip. She wasn't surprised when the tour wound through many of the same ceramics shops they'd visited before.

Nancy wondered if Hiro would take them to the studio where Theo Meredith worked, or if it would even be open. If the studio really was concealing stolen pearls in their vases, and the Kyoto police were investigating, the studio might have shut down for good.

In any case, she realized, I've got to get there soon. What little energy she'd had that morning was almost completely gone. Despite the fact that her case wasn't solved, Nancy only wanted to lie down and sleep.

She was so exhausted that she didn't even notice when Hiro led them past a familiar *torii* gate and toward the studio where Lettie Aldridge had bought her vase.

"Nancy," Bess whispered, "it's open!"

Nancy nodded, trying to fight off the fuzziness in her head. Now that they were there, what exactly did she plan to do? Theo was going to recognize them, she realized, and there wasn't much she could do about that.

They entered the low doorway that led into the shop, and Nancy smiled for the first time all day. Listening intently to Theo Meredith explain ancient glazing techniques were Frank and Joe Hardy.

Frank was soon at Nancy's side. "You should be back in the hotel," he scolded gently.

Nancy ignored the remark. "You know," she whispered, "the only part of the studio they don't show you is what's behind that little wooden door in the back wall."

"It's probably some sort of storeroom," Frank whispered back, following her gaze. "You'd like to have a look, wouldn't you?" he guessed.

"You bet I would," she told him.

With a grin, Frank said, "Mmm. Let's see what we can do about that." He gave a hand signal to Joe.

Seconds later Joe was doubled over on the floor of the studio. "My knee!" he howled. "It's gone out! Quick, someone get help fast. *Ooooh,* it hurts!"

Nancy watched, amused, as everyone gathered around Joe—except Frank. Frank was carefully opening the wood door Nancy had pointed out. Nancy didn't want to draw attention to Frank, so she, too, focused on Joe.

A minute later everyone was still gathered around Joe when Frank slipped back out of the storeroom and past Nancy. She backed inconspicuously away from the group, then followed him onto the street.

Frank winked and reached inside his denim jacket. Then he handed Nancy one of the blue-and-white vases. "Take this back to Tokyo as quickly as you can," he said. "We'll sort it out there. I'd go with you, but I'm afraid the others will get suspicious if I don't start looking concerned about Joe. Go ahead. I'll make some explanation to Bess and Hiro."

Nancy nodded. "Thanks, Frank. You guys are the greatest. See you back at the hotel."

Nancy was about a block from the ceramics studio, just passing the tall *torii* that led into the Shinto shrine she'd noticed earlier, when she heard Frank's voice behind her. "Run, Nancy!" he shouted. "Don't look back, just run!"

Nancy picked up her pace, glancing hurriedly over her shoulder. Theo Meredith was racing toward her, his face red with fury. A good distance behind him was Hiro, trailed by the Hardys and Bess.

Hoping she'd find help in the Shinto shrine, Nancy ran beneath the *torii.* After all, it had worked at the Buddhist temple. Ahead of her a steep grass-covered hill led up to the shrine. There was no one in sight. Any priests were probably up near the temple buildings.

Desperation gave her a burst of energy, and Nancy forced herself uphill. But the drug was still in her system, and the energy didn't last. Soon she was fighting for every breath.

Winded and exhausted, she stumbled. The vase fell from her hand, hit the ground, and split in two. Dozens of shimmering white pearls rolled into the grass at her feet. Nancy stared down at them, too spent to feel triumphant.

The sound of someone else breathing hard made her raise her head. Theo Meredith walked toward her, a knife balanced comfortably in one hand.

"Move away from the vase," he ordered. "I can see you're not feeling very well, but don't worry. In a minute you won't feel anything at all."

Chapter Twenty-One

NANCY CLOSED HER HAND around one of the broken pieces of pottery and got to her feet. "So you're the mastermind behind this?" she asked, backing away from Theo Meredith. Somehow she had to stall for time.

Theo bowed his head modestly. "Among others."

"How did you get pearls inside the vases without firing them?" Nancy asked.

"A very ancient technique," Theo replied mockingly. "A false bottom glued to each vase."

"And then you sold the vases to seniors on the Journeys East tours," Nancy said, stating what she'd already guessed.

Theo bowed again. "And wrapped them in boxes with a red seal on the bottom. Then, when our seniors passed safely through U.S. customs with the vases, the Journeys bus driver would switch the boxes with identical boxes—containing identical vases *without* pearls."

So *that* was how the pearls were recovered in the States, Nancy thought. It was almost too easy—and too devious.

"And the identical ones were stored in the hotel linen closet," Nancy concluded, "the ones that didn't contain smuggled pearls."

Theo nodded. "It was all very neat. The seniors got pretty ceramics, and we got our pearls. No one was the wiser until *you* came along."

Nancy didn't like the way this conversation was going. Where were the others? she wondered, but she didn't dare look and call attention to them.

"You broke into our room at the inn," Nancy accused.

Theo smiled smugly at her. "Let's just say a friend did it for me. I couldn't let you walk off with one of our special vases, now could I?"

"And you had us trailed by the *yakuza!*"

"Enough questions," Theo said abruptly. He edged toward her, and sunlight glinted off the knife in his hand.

Nancy backed away, swaying slightly. Theo was holding the knife lightly but close to his body, the way a street fighter would. And she remembered what she'd learned about street fighters in self-defense class—they were unpredictable and deadly.

She clutched the jagged piece of pottery in her hand, knowing it was a poor defense. Besides, she was feeling so weak, she probably wouldn't be able to use it effectively.

For a split second Nancy took her eyes off Theo. Hiro and the others were about thirty yards away. Now was the time to distract Theo.

"Hiro's coming after you," she warned, still backing away.

Theo smiled. "I'm terrified," he said sarcastically, without taking his eyes off her.

Out of the corner of her eye, Nancy saw Frank burst ahead of the others. "I've already called the police," she lied, trying to keep Theo's attention off Frank.

"Really?" Theo asked. "They'll have—" He was cut off as Frank dove full out and took him down in a powerful tackle. The two wrestled, struggling for control of the knife. Theo drove his arm upward, stabbing wildly, but Frank managed to hold his wrist away.

Nancy watched, terrified, as the two fought, the blade edging closer and closer to Frank. With a tremendous surge of energy Frank finally knocked the knife free. As the two got to their feet and continued to fight, Nancy stumbled toward the knife. She knew she ought to pick it up or at least kick it out of the way.

"Don't touch it!" Hiro commanded in a harsh voice Nancy barely recognized. She looked up and saw him standing there, his body in a calm, easy fighting stance. In his eyes was the coldest, hardest look Nancy had ever seen.

Suddenly she understood why Theo hadn't been afraid of Hiro. Hiro wasn't after Theo. He was after *her.* Her suspicions about him must have been correct—Hiro *was* involved with the pearl smuggling.

Nancy watched as Hiro went to Theo's aid, picking Frank off with a spinning back kick that sent Frank stumbling backward. He landed hard on the ground. Nancy's heart sank as she watched him struggle to sit up while Theo advanced, ready to finish him off.

"No!" Joe shouted.

Nancy's eyes widened as Joe launched himself at Theo. Although Joe was moving stiffly, he managed to connect with a solid punch, and Theo went down. Nancy didn't have time to feel relief, however, because now Joe was facing Hiro.

Hiro was every bit as deadly as she'd suspected. He lashed out with a series of lightning strikes that left Joe on the ground, moaning.

Nancy gulped as Hiro turned to her. He wasn't even breathing hard.

"Why didn't you stay in Tokyo today?" he asked.

In a flash of insight, everything became clear to Nancy. "You're the one who knocked me out last night and poisoned me," she accused.

"I was very careful not to kill you," he informed her.

Nancy couldn't believe it—he was actually acting as if he expected her to be grateful! "Why did you tell Bess that we should go to Kyoto?" she asked. "You almost guaranteed that we'd find the ceramics shop!"

"Bess said you'd been talking about pearls with Lettie," Hiro said. "I had to know if you were really investigating."

"So you set us up at the *ryokan* and had us watched."

Hiro nodded. "And then I did everything in my power to scare you off. But you couldn't take a warning, could you? This time you leave me no choice."

Nancy's heart was hammering. She knew that when the attack came, she wouldn't even see him move. He was that fast.

Suddenly Hiro was in the air, launched in a flying side kick.

In the same instant, Bess was in front of Nancy, shielding her friend with her body. "Hiro, no!" Bess screamed.

To Nancy's amazement, a look of horror

crossed Hiro's face. Nancy didn't know how he could move so fast, but he managed to pull back the kick. Instead of hurting Bess, he landed awkwardly on his side.

Nancy could barely follow what happened next. Gary shouted, "Wendy, get the police!" Then there was a mad scuffle as Gary fell on top of Hiro, followed by Frank, Joe, and Margot.

Hiro fought viciously for a moment and then stopped, clearly overpowered.

Aside from Wendy, who was summoning help, there was one member of the group who wasn't holding Hiro down. Michael Ryder was standing off to the side, taping the entire thing.

The next afternoon Joe had settled himself on the couch in their Tokyo apartment. Nancy, Bess, and Frank sat crowded around the tiny kitchen table a few feet away. "Spacious apartment, huh?" Joe asked.

"Very roomy," Nancy agreed, smiling. She nodded toward the print on the wall. "And a great view of your favorite mountain." She glanced at Joe curiously. "Did you ever find out who pushed you?"

Joe sat up straighter on the couch. "One of Kamura's thugs, the guy with the *bo,* confessed to it. Kamura had him planted up there, just off the trail, waiting for me."

Frank stood over his brother, hands on hips. "Are you sure you should be sitting up?"

"Frank," Joe said patiently, "I'm bruised, not dying of a terminal disease. Now stop hovering and relax." He glanced at Nancy, who seemed to be fully recovered from the events of the last two days. There was color in her cheeks now, and she was animated and alert. "How are you feeling?" Joe asked her.

"Perfect," she said, smiling. "The doctor called with the results of the blood test. Hiro knocked me out with a common prescription sedative mixed with alcohol. She said that in a higher dosage it might have been lethal. But since Hiro was so careful, it just took a day to get it out of my system."

Joe saw Bess flinch at the mention of Hiro. Now that he thought about it, Bess hadn't said a single word since she and Nancy had arrived at the apartment. For Bess, that had to mean something was seriously wrong.

"Hey, are you all right?" he asked her gently.

"I just can't believe Hiro was mixed up in all this," Bess said. "How could he be working with a *yakuza?*"

"According to the police, they were high school friends in Kyoto," Nancy answered. "They met before the *yakuza* became a *yakuza.*"

"So he was the one who stole the pearls from the Kii peninsula?" Frank asked.

Nancy nodded. "And Hiro and Kenji came up with a plan for how they could smuggle the stolen pearls into the States and sell them there."

Bess stood up and began pacing the tiny apartment, her voice outraged. "He sent a *yakuza* to break into our room, and to follow us—"

"Actually, it was Theo who arranged that," Nancy explained. "But they were all in it together. Remember, Hiro made the arrangements for us to stay at the *ryokan.* He warned Theo that we'd probably show up at the ceramics studio. I think we were being watched the entire time we were in Kyoto."

"And the police haven't found any trace of the *yakuza?"* Joe asked.

Nancy shook her head. "He's the only one they haven't got. But they've confiscated all the vases from the seniors. Five of them contained pearls."

"What I still don't get," Frank said, "is Isao's part in all this. Joe originally saw the *yakuza* with Isao, and I heard Isao say something to Mariko about pearls. What's the connection?"

"Why don't you ask Mariko?" Joe said, smiling. "I called her last night. She'll be here any moment."

As Joe had predicted, Mariko Yamada arrived a few minutes later. What he hadn't expected was that her uncle would be with her. "Mr. Yamada," he said, trying to keep the surprise out of his voice, "what are you doing back so soon?"

Mr. Yamada nodded toward Frank. "After our last phone call, when I realized Amsa employees were trying to kill you two, it seemed imperative that I return. I caught the first flight back to Tokyo.

"Fortunately for him, the police got to Tadashi Kamura before I did," Mr. Yamada went on, "but I've had extensive discussions with Mr. Okata and Isao Matsuda."

"And?" Frank asked, looking expectantly at the older man.

"To my great relief Mr. Okata was not involved in the counterfeiting. I have always thought that he is one of our most loyal employees. I am happy I was not wrong."

"He just let Kamura get away with it," Joe said bitterly.

Mr. Yamada sighed. "Please try to understand. Okata regarded Kamura as a protégé. Even now he has trouble believing that Kamura could be involved in something so dishonorable. He sent Kamura down the mountain with you simply because Kamura was the person he trusted most. Of us all, Okata may be the one who was most deeply betrayed."

Joe glanced at Bess again, silently disagreeing.

"I have also spoken with Mr. Hamaguchi," Yamada went on. "He had no part in the counterfeiting, either."

"What about Isao?" Frank looked at Mariko. "I heard him say something to you on the mountain about pearls."

Mariko rolled her eyes. "He kept trying to sell me a pearl necklace. Can you believe it?" She glanced down at the short, electric blue dress she was wearing. "I mean, pearls aren't even my style."

"That's what you two were talking about the day I saw you in the hall?" Joe asked.

Mariko laughed. "That was the first offer. Then he kept pulling me aside to give me lower and lower prices."

"Where would Isao Matsuda get a pearl necklace?" Frank wondered aloud.

Mariko gave Joe a haughty glance. "You're not the only one who can put clues together, you know. The jewelry came from the *yakuza,* who happens to be Isao's cousin."

"The necklace must have been one of the sample pieces that were stolen from the pearl farm," Nancy said. "I bet that's what Isao gave—or sold—to that sumo wrestler."

"He told the police they were earrings for the wrestler's girlfriend," Mr. Yamada said. "By the way, that wrestler is no longer with the stable. They said he was always a discipline problem."

"What's going to happen to Isao now?" Joe asked. He felt sorry for the nervous boy.

"The police are holding him on charges of selling stolen goods," Yamada replied. "I'm glad he wasn't mixed up in the counterfeiting as well."

"So," Joe said slowly, "the counterfeiting operation was Kamura's brainchild."

Mr. Yamada nodded. "But even he made mistakes—for example, leaving classified schematics on his desk. He was extremely confident and extremely arrogant."

"Even when he knew I was onto him," Mariko added.

Joe looked at her, and suddenly all his old exasperation at Mariko returned. "What exactly were you doing?" he demanded. "Playing detective or trying to get yourself kicked out of the trainee program?"

Mariko's face flushed. "Both," she said quietly. Then she lifted her face and gazed proudly at her uncle. "I didn't want to come to Tokyo and be reformed into a passive Japanese woman."

Her uncle gave her a wry smile. "I think there was little danger of that."

"And I didn't want to be a good little Amsa

trainee," she went on. "They all act like company clones. So, yes, I was trying to get kicked out of the program and sent home."

"But—" Joe said.

"But believe it or not," Mariko went on before Joe could finish, "I didn't want my uncle to hate me." She took a deep breath and continued, "When I realized that the schematics on Kamura's desk were for the top secret video cartridges, I figured that meant he was somehow undermining Amsa. So I decided I'd find out what he was doing. Then I thought maybe my uncle would respect me for being who I am."

"Mariko," Mr. Yamada's voice was a soft rebuke, "this is not the time nor the place for this discussion. But I assure you, my niece, I have loved and respected you since you were a child."

"To our last night in Tokyo." Gary Leontes lifted his glass in a toast.

Nancy lifted her glass, too, looking around the table at Gary, Bess, Mariko, and the Hardys. The teens had all decided to eat a delicious sushi dinner at the hotel for their last meal. Now they lingered at the table. Nancy had the feeling that no one was quite ready to say goodbye.

Gary nodded at the Hardys, "So you two are flying home tomorrow, too?"

"Yup," Joe told him.

"And you, Mariko?" Nancy asked.

"My uncle and I had a long talk, and—I've agreed to finish out my trainee program." She winked at Joe. "Won't Mr. Okata be thrilled?"

While the others bantered back and forth, Nancy gazed worriedly at Bess. Out of everyone, Bess was the only one who wasn't in good spirits. Nancy knew Bess had been trying to make the best of things. She'd even made a valiant effort to look as if she enjoyed dinner. Now she was playing nervously with her napkin, oblivious to the good-natured joking of the others.

"Still thinking about Hiro?" Nancy guessed.

"I can't help it," Bess said. 'I still care about him, but every time I think about him, I come up with another crummy thing he did. He's the one who sent you that warning note, wasn't he?"

"Actually that was Wendy," Nancy told her.

"But the first warning—"

"She meant the fortune-teller," Gary cut in. "I had a talk with Wendy, and she confessed everything."

"Why would she threaten Nancy?" Bess asked.

Gary looked embarrassed. "Wendy thought Nancy and I were getting too close. She thought that she and I should be a couple even though I've told her it would never work out."

"Nothing works out," Bess said morosely. "I keep asking myself why I didn't see through Hiro. The whole time we were together we had such a good time."

"No one else saw through him either," Gary reminded her. "We all thought he was a great guy."

"He really did care for you," Nancy said gently. "You were the reason he stopped his attack. I don't know what he would have done to me, but he couldn't bear to hurt you."

"He would have hurt you," Bess said, "and I can't get past that."

"Please excuse us for interrupting your dinner," a deep voice said next to their table.

Nancy was startled to see two police officers standing there. Each officer was holding two wrapped packages.

"Nancy Drew, Bess Marvin, and Frank and Joe Hardy?" one of the officers asked.

The four friends nodded.

"The concierge said you might be here. We have brought you a small token of our appreciation for helping us solve two difficult cases." The officers held out the packages.

"You first," Frank said, smiling at Nancy.

Nancy couldn't hold back a groan of disbelief

as she unwrapped her gift. Inside was a very familiar blue-and-white ceramic vase.

"Any pearls inside?" Bess asked, grinning.

"I'm afraid not," the first officer said.

"Perfect," Nancy said, her blue eyes sparkling with mischief. "I've been looking for a vase like this for my aunt . . ."